Under HER

OTHER CONTEMPORARY NOVELS BY SAMANTHA TOWLE

Wardrobe Malfunction
Unsuitable
Sacking the Quarterback (BookShots Flames/James Patterson)
The Ending I Want
When I Was Yours
Trouble

REVVED SERIES

Revved
Revived

THE STORM SERIES

The Mighty Storm
Wethering the Storm
Taming the Storm
The Storm

PARANORMAL ROMANCES BY SAMANTHA TOWLE

The Bringer

THE ALEXANDRA JONES SERIES

First Bitten
Original Sin

Under
HER

SAMANTHA TOWLE

Copyright © 2017 by Samantha Towle
All rights reserved.

Visit my website at http://samanthatowle.co.uk
Cover Designer: Najla Qamber Designs
Editor and Interior Designer: Jovana Shirley,
Unforeseen Editing, www.unforeseenediting.com

No part of this book may be reproduced or transmitted in any form or by any means, electronic or mechanical, including photocopying, recording, or by any information storage and retrieval system without the written permission of the author, except for the use of brief quotations in a book review.

This book is a work of fiction. Names, characters, places, and incidents either are products of the author's imagination or are used fictitiously. Any resemblance to actual persons, living or dead, events, or locales is entirely coincidental.

ISBN-13: 987-1974499052

"Good morning, Mr. Cross."

Leah, our new receptionist's, singsong voice dances across the lobby from her spot at the sleek reception desk. I can see her legs under the desk. Her skirt has run up her thighs, and she's wearing stockings.

I know this little show is for my benefit. Like it has been every day since she started. A different seduction technique, but it's not escaped my radar that Leah wants to fuck me.

Of course she does. I'm hot and rich as fuck. And I'm also the boss. And the soon-to-be CEO of my family's company, Under Her Lingerie, when my parents retire and hand the reins over to me.

That's right. I sell underwear. Sexy-as-fuck underwear. The very thing that I love to peel off a woman's body right before I screw her senseless.

I have the best job in the world.

"Good morning, Leah." I give her a brief, pleasant smile. Not the smile I know can get women into bed or on their knees for me in minutes.

No flirting back with Leah because she works for me.

Rule number one: Never fuck the staff.

I don't want or need the complications that sleeping with an employee would bring.

Aside from leaving myself wide open for a lawsuit and that my mother would kill me for dipping my pen in the company ink, I can't deal with the drama and tears when she clues in to the fact that all I wanted from her was sex.

Even though I would have repeatedly told her that it was a one-time thing.

That's rule number two: Always make it clear that hook-ups are just that.

Rule number three: Never let them know where you live, work, or what your phone number is just in case rule number two doesn't stick.

I press the call button for the elevator, and the door opens immediately. I get on and hit the button for the fourteenth floor where my office is.

I fucking love this building. It's home to me. Everyone here is like family. My parents like to run a happy ship, and they treat their employees very well. My folks are well loved. They are the best. I know everyone here is sad to see them retire. There were a lot of tears the day it was announced.

Honestly, it will be weird for me, being here and running this place without them.

But I'm excited, too. This is what I've been working toward my whole life.

The elevator arrives on my floor, and I step out when the door opens. I walk through the lobby and toward the executive offices, and then I push open the door to my office area.

My PA, Chrissy, is already at her desk.

Under HER

She lifts her head from her screen. "Morning, Wilder." She picks up my takeout coffee from her desk, which she brings in for me every day, and holds it out.

She's the best PA ever. I'm lucky to have her.

"Thanks." I take the coffee and have a sip. I love my coffee hot, to the point of almost burning. How the hell people can drink lukewarm coffee is beyond me. The hotter, the better. Just how I like my women.

"Good weekend?" she asks me.

"Of course." I grin.

Don't get me wrong. I fucking love my job, but weekends are reserved solely for playtime, and I love playing.

Friday night was spent between the legs of Ida, a Swedish supermodel I'd met at a show a few weeks ago. Saturday night was boys' night out with my buddies, Cooper and Dominic. The three of us go out every Saturday night, and we end it with each of us in a different chick's bed.

I am in no way ready to settle down with just one woman. I don't have anything against relationships per se. I just don't want one.

Well, not at the moment anyway. I like—no, I fucking *love* my life.

I love my job. And I love having a different woman in bed with me every weekend. I get to have regular sex without the demands and complications of a relationship, as there are always plenty of women willing to service my needs. But I'm not a selfish bastard. I like to make sure that the woman I'm screwing is having a good time. I can't get off if she doesn't.

I'm a total boss at oral sex. I've had a lot of practice. I fucking love going down on a woman. There's nothing better to get me going than that first taste of a woman's pussy.

I have a perfect setup.

Sex is reserved for weekends because the week is for work.

Work always comes first, and I don't see that changing anytime soon. Especially not now that I'll be taking over the running of the company from my parents.

Maybe, in the distant future—like ten or fifteen years—I'll meet some girl I want to have a relationship with, but if I'm being totally honest, I just can't see it happening.

And, really, it would be grossly unfair to the women of Chicago if I took myself off the market. My dick is just too awesome to keep to one woman.

Sundays are brunch with the boys, so we can talk about the escapades from the night before, and then I usually spend the rest of Sunday working from home, getting ready for Monday morning.

"How was yours?" I know she was going to Milwaukee to spend the weekend with her fiancée's parents.

Yes, *fiancée*, as in another woman. Chrissy is gay, and she's getting married to a woman called Wendy. And, no, she's not your stereotypical butch or porno-hot lesbian.

She's just a normal, good-looking woman. And she runs my life like a champ.

"Yeah, it was okay, but Wendy and her mom were talking wedding stuff nonstop all weekend."

She rolls her eyes, and I laugh.

"Anyway, I've got this morning's schedule ready for you, but first, your mom and dad are waiting for you in your office."

"They are?" I move my eyes in the direction of my office door.

"Yep."

"How long have they been waiting?"

"Only five minutes or so."

"And they didn't say what they wanted to see me for?"

"Nope."

A mild unease settles in my gut.

Of course, it's not unusual for my parents to turn up in my office unannounced, but first thing in the morning is unusual.

The last time they were waiting in my office for me this early in the morning was seven years ago when I was in a much smaller, much shittier office, working in the sales department, and I'd just screwed up the Renshaw deal. The big deal that they'd trusted me with.

And, by screwed up, I mean, I'd screwed Mr. Renshaw's daughter, Amber, a few months prior.

In my defense, I hadn't known who she was then, and the deal was in its infancy at that point.

But the problem was, Amber had wanted more than one ride on my dick, and when I'd told her—as I'd told her before we boned down—that it was a one-off, she hadn't been so happy at all.

Like took-her-high-heeled-shoe-off-and-threw-it-at-my-head not happy. I was lucky I hadn't lost an eye.

Seriously, why is it that some women will agree to no-strings sex, and then once the sex is over, they completely forget the prior conversation?

I know my dick is awesome, but he doesn't have mind-erasing skills.

I don't have time for relationships. And I like my life the way it is. Sex with no strings.

But Amber had been at the dinner meeting with Mr. Renshaw, and she had taken one look at me, whispered something in her father's ear, and that was the end of that. Renshaw had decided he no longer was interested in considering stocking our products in his department stores. Well, he hadn't exactly put it that politely, but you can imagine what he'd said.

I get that she's his daughter, but it's not my fault that she's batshit crazy. And, seriously, if the guy can't detach business from personal, then we shouldn't want to work with him anyway.

But my parents didn't exactly see it that way.

I got reamed out for losing the deal and also a lecture from my mom about how I should be treating women with respect and not trying to sleep my way through Chicago.

But that was seven years ago, and even though it still bugs me that it was the one deal I fucked up, I have to allow myself the fact that I was wet behind the ears in business. Everyone is allowed one screwup in business.

But I didn't let the Renshaw fiasco put me off. I like fucking way too much to stop having it on the regular.

I just had to learn to be a lot smarter about who I climbed into bed with, which means that I make sure to keep my weekend activities far, far away from anything associated with the office. One sniff of a business connection with a potential screw, and I'm out of there and on to the next.

Maybe my parents just want to talk about the takeover. My parents will be retiring in a few weeks, and I'll be taking over as CEO.

I know what you're thinking. I'm their son, and that's why they are giving me the job.

Wrong.

My parents are hard-asses. We might have money, but they've made me work for everything. My parents came from nothing and built this business together, and they want me to understand that you have to work hard in this life if you want anything. Nothing is just handed to you.

I had part-time jobs throughout high school, so long as they didn't interfere with my studies. The only time I didn't work was when I was in college, as my parents wanted me to focus fully on my studies. But every summer was spent here, in the office, working for them—whether it was in the mailroom or on reception. I've worked my ass off to learn this business inside out.

I did four years at Northwestern, earning a business degree. And then I went off to Columbia where I got my

MBA in management. When I graduated from Columbia, I came back home to Chicago and started working here in sales. I have worked in every department in the company so that I will understand the running of the business for when it is my time to take over.

And now is my time.

"Wish me luck," I say to Chrissy.

"You don't need it, Mr. Soon-to-Be CEO." She says the last part on a whisper even though no one is around to hear.

When my parents announced their retirement a month ago, it wasn't formally announced that I'd be taking over. Everyone probably already knows though. I mean, it's a given.

That must be why they're in there, waiting—to talk about the big announcement.

I don't get excited about much, but I'm excited about this.

With thoughts of my impending CEO status, I open the door to my office with a big fucking smile on my face.

"Mom, Dad," I greet them both.

They're sitting on my black leather sofa. I fucking love my office. It's big with floor-to-ceiling windows, so the view of the city is immense. And I have my own private bathroom, which is always a bonus.

"Wilder." My mom smiles warmly. "How are you doing?"

"I'm good. What can I do for you this morning?" I ask as I walk the distance over to my desk.

A brief silence hangs in the air. That silence makes my gut tighten.

Then, my dad says, "We need to have a chat."

"Okay." I lower my ass into my chair.

They turn in their seats to face me. I don't like what I see on their faces—unease.

Fuck.

I take a drink of my coffee, needing the burn to steady me, before lowering it to the desk. "What's up?" I ask, forcing my voice to remain steady.

"Well…" My dad clears his throat.

"We have news," Mom imparts, a fake cheeriness to her voice.

They're not retiring. They've changed their minds.
Double fuck.

And me wanting them to retire does not make me a bad son or selfish. My parents have worked hard their whole lives, building this business up and making it into what it is today. But they're in their late sixties, and I want them to take it easy and enjoy their golden years.

"Good or bad news?" My eyes flicker between the pair of them, trying to catch anything in their expressions, but they're giving away nothing.

"Good news." Mom beams a smile. "Isn't it, Frank?" She nudges my dad in the side with her elbow.

He grunts a sound that she gives a disapproving look to. And that sound does nothing to appease the sick feeling I have right now.

"Now, honey, even though this is good news, I have a feeling you might not think so off the bat, but I just want you to have an open mind and listen to what we have to say."

"Okay…" *I'm so not okay.*

"Well, there's no other way to say this than to just say it, so…we've hired another CEO to come work here with you and help you run the company."

"I'm sorry, what?" I'm pretty sure I'm having a stroke. I rub a hand over my frozen face and then stare over at my mom. "You're gonna have to say that again because, for a second there…I thought you said that you'd hired another…CEO."

"I did. And we have."

F*uck. Fuck. Fuck.*
I stare at my mom's steady face. My eyes move to my dad's face. His expression is blank, giving me nothing.

"Is this a joke?"

"No," my mother says softly. It's the voice she used when I was younger and I was upset, and she was trying to soothe me.

The pacifying voice.

I used to love that voice. Now, I officially hate it.

"Why the fuck did you do that?"

"Language, Wilder," my mom chastises.

Like now is the time to quibble over my use of the English language.

My wide eyes go to my dad. "Am I not getting the job?"

I see a flash of dismay in his eyes. "Of course you are," my dad says, his tone resolute. "The job is yours, Wild. Without a doubt. Your mom just thought—"

"We *both* think"—my mom flashes a stern look at my dad—"that you could do with the support that having a co-CEO would offer. It's a lot of work, running a business of this size."

"I know. And I'm fully equipped and ready to do so. That's what you've been training me to do for the past seven years. Jesus, I've been working toward this ever since I started coming in with you both when I was a kid. I know this business inside and out! No one knows the lingerie business better than I do." I'm getting louder and louder, but I can't help it.

A co-CEO. A motherfucking co-CEO!

"Wilder, we know how experienced and knowledgeable you are. It's not about that. Your dad and I have successfully run this company *together*. Lots of companies nowadays have co-CEOs. There are a lot of benefits in having a partner to run the company with."

I want to have an actual honest-to-God tantrum. Throw my toys out of my crib. Yell at them that they're wrong. That I could run this company with one arm tied behind my back while blindfolded. I want to pull the how-could-you-do-this-to-your-own-kid card. It might work on my dad, but I know it wouldn't work on my mom. She's a tough cookie. My throwing a hissy fit would only reinforce to them that they made the right decision to hire this new person to come and work here with me.

No, what I have to do is be mature about this.

Tell them that I'm dismayed that they did this. Not pissed. Dismayed. Especially because they went about it all covertly and behind my back.

But I'll make sure to work with this new co-fucking-CEO asshole and be nice as pie.

And, in reality, I'll be looking for a way to get rid of this job-stealing asshole while proving that I'm more than capable of running the company alone. *My* company.

Under HER

I take a calming deep breath and place my hands, palms down, on my desk. "Well, I can't say that I'm happy about this turn of events because I'm not. But it's your company, and you're free to do as you please with it. Yes, I'm your son—your *only* child—and heir. But you raised me right, and I'll go along with whatever you think is best for the company." Okay, so I'm laying it on a little thick, but a man's gotta do what a man's gotta do, and guilt is the only card I have to play here.

"Wilder, I know you're thinking that we made this decision to bring someone else in because we think you can't run the company alone. But that's not the case."

"I'm not thinking that at all. I know I'm more than capable of running the company alone." My surly words echo my thoughts.

Okay, so my attempt to guilt trip them didn't last very long, and that smart comment is definitely not going to help my cause, but I just couldn't help it.

At my tenacity, I see a small smile touch my dad's lips, which tells me this was more my mother's idea than his. That gives me a boost, knowing that he's not one hundred percent on board with this, so he'll be easier to sway when the time comes.

"Of course you are, Wilder. But what's made this company so successful is the male-female dynamic from your father and me."

"So, from that, should I take it that you've hired a woman?"

"Yes. We've hired a female co-CEO to help you run the company. I love you, Wilder. You're my son. You're incredibly bright and talented. But, when it comes to women, you don't have a clue. You don't understand their wants and needs."

I'm mortally offended by this. I know women's needs very well, but it's not like I can vocalize this to my mom. I mean, no guy wants to share his sexual expertise with his mother.

My brow goes up. "That's a very sexist thing for you to say, Mom."

My dad smothers a laugh.

My mom throws an annoyed glance at my dad and then looks back at me, her brows furrowed in annoyance. "I meant that you don't understand their wants and needs when it comes to the actual items. That can only come from being a woman. And having both a male and female viewpoint helps enormously with the business we're in. My view comes from a woman's perspective—of actually wearing and understanding the product, the issues of materials and comfort as well as the look. Your father's perspective is in sales and focused on branding. Together, we've been a formidable team. I want that for you."

"I'm not marrying this chick."

"Of course not!" My mother's laugh tinkles around the room.

"Your mother just wants you to have a counterbalance, Wilder," my dad says.

"Why didn't you tell me this before now?"

"Because we weren't sure that we were going to find the right person to fit the role."

"And, now, you have?"

"Yes."

"Just out of curiosity, what would you have done if you hadn't found the right woman for the job?"

My mother's shoulders lift. "We would have crossed that bridge when we came to it."

I know my parents love me, but this sure does feel a lot like betrayal, and it tastes bitter as fuck.

"We're not doing this to hurt you, Wilder. You know we've only ever had your best interests at heart."

"Mmhmm." I fold my arms over my chest. "And how long will I be co-CEOing for?"

My mom's brows draw together. "What do you mean?"

"I mean, how long will I have to share my job for?"

My parents glance at each other and then back at me.

"Well, we're not sure...exactly," my mom answers.

"So, that means, I will one day have the company to run alone?"

My mother looks at my father again. But he's looking at me.

"Yes," he says decisively. "Wilder, you know the company will be yours when your mother and I are gone. And you can do as you choose with it then."

"Well, I'm hoping you don't go anytime soon, and I'd quite like to run the business solo well before then."

"Let's put a pin in this for now." My mother claps her hands together, ending the conversation.

Put a pin in it? Jesus fucking Christ. We're talking about my life here, and my mom wants to stick a pin in it.

But I know that pushing the issue right now will get me nowhere. I need to tackle this again—and soon—but at this moment in time, I need to deal with the crap they've just dropped in my lap.

"So, when do I get to meet this mystery woman?" *Who's stealing half of my company.*

Okay, she's not actually stealing it, but she's definitely stealing half of my job.

"Tomorrow."

"Tomorrow," I echo.

"Yes, she's coming in first thing tomorrow morning to meet with you. And then, afterward, in the weekly meeting, we'll formally announce her new role along with your step up as co-CEOs."

Co-CEO. The word makes me want to vomit.

If I didn't love my parents, I would legit strangle them right now. With my bare hands.

A day. I've got a motherfucking day to get my head around this...this curveball that they've thrown at me.

"I know you're worried about this, Wilder, but Morgan is great, and you do actually already know her," my mom says.

That brings my head up. "I know her?"

Please God don't let it be someone I slept with. Not that I do much sleeping with the women I have sex with. I'm not one to hang around after the deed is done.

"Morgan told us that you went to Northwestern together," my dad says.

Morgan. Northwestern. Went together.

This isn't sounding good.

And knowing my fuck rate at Northwestern, my odds of not having screwed this chick are diminishing by the second.

I swallow past the dryness in my throat. "What's her surname?"

"Stickford," Mom says. "Morgan Stickford."

Ah, hell.

Morgan Stick-Up-Her-Ass-Ford.

Relief and dismay sweep through me in equal measure.

Relief because I definitely didn't sleep with her in college.

Dismay because she hated me in college.

Which was a shame because she was a pretty thing. Well, her face was, which was always on show—as her hair was habitually tied back into a ponytail—unlike her body, which was always covered up with ugly-ass big sweaters.

And she was so damn serious all the time. Hence the nickname Stick-Up-Her-Ass-Ford.

She never went to parties. She spent all her time either in the library or with her nose stuck up the professors' asses.

I never once heard of her socializing or saw her with any friends. She was a stuck-up bitch who thought that she was better than everyone else. Me included.

Under Her

Morgan Stickford took an instant dislike to me from the word *go* without even bothering to get to know me.

She came to the conclusion that I was an overprivileged, womanizing man-whore.

Okay, so I did have certain privileges growing up because of my parents' success, and, yes, I had a job to walk straight into out of college, but believe me, my parents made me work for it. Nothing has ever been handed to me. I've earned everything I have.

And, sure, I liked ass. I still do. But, back then, I was young and horny. Hot college girls were everywhere, and I made sure to screw almost all of them.

Except for her.

Because she took one look at me and thought she had me pegged. When, in actuality, she knew fuck all about me.

Did it annoy the shit out of me? Sure, it did. But I wasn't going to lose sleep over a stuck-up bitch who went around and made snap judgments about people she barely knew.

But then that was nine years ago. A lot can change in nine years. Maybe Morgan Stickford has changed.

Well, I hope to fuck she has because, for the short-term—until I get rid of her—I'm stuck with sharing my company with her.

3

Even though I had a shitload of work to get through today, I couldn't focus on anything after the nuclear bomb my parents had dropped on me.

So, I did what every other person in my position would do.

I stalked Morgan online.

I might have known her back in college—not that I really knew her that well—but I definitely don't know Morgan now.

I don't know what she's been up to in the last nine years. Or if she's still a massive bitch.

And do you know what I got for spending my day researching her?

Fuck. All.

She doesn't have a Twitter or Instagram account. She does have a Facebook account—well, if it's hers. I could only find one account for a Morgan Stickford in Chicago.

But that was locked down tight—just like her legs had been in college—so I figured it had to be her.

After my unsuccessful Morgan stalking, I sent the boys an SOS text and asked them to meet me at Doyle's. It's an Irish pub that's popular with the after-work crowd. I like it there. The feel is laid-back, and the food is great. Not that I feel like eating. But drinking? I definitely feel like drinking. That shows how stressed I am. I rarely drink during the week.

I push through the door into Doyle's. I see Cooper's already here, sitting at the bar, sipping on a beer.

Coop is my oldest friend. Even though I'm tight with Dom, Coop is my best friend. I've known him since high school. Went to Northwestern with me, which is where we met Dom. But Coop hadn't needed to go to college. He's richer than I am. I'm pretty sure he's richer than God. He comes from old money.

I'm sure you've heard of Delaney's. The big-ass supermarket chain.

Coop is the heir to Delaney's. His great-grandpa started the business way back when, which he passed on to Coop's grandpa. Coop's mom was Grandpa Delaney's only kid. And all she did was spend Grandpa Delaney's money and get knocked up by Coop's dad. Weird thing is, no one knows who Coop's dad is. His mom has never said. To this day, Coop still doesn't know. His mom's a selfish bitch. She was hardly there while Coop was growing up; she was too busy traveling the world and finding the next man to marry. She's been married eight times. I shit you not.

Grandpa Delaney raised Coop. Sadly, he died of lung cancer when Coop was sixteen. Coop didn't take it well. He took it even worse when he found out that Grandpa Delaney had left him everything. He was sixteen and clueless. So, a CEO was brought in to run the company until Coop was ready to step into his rightful place.

He never has.

Under HER

After he graduated college, he just bummed around for a bit. He still kind of does. He spends his days sleeping and his nights partying and screwing beautiful woman and getting his name in the gossip columns on a regular basis.

I think he's capable of so much more. No, I *know* he's capable of more. But I don't push the issue. He's my best friend, and it's his decision how he chooses to run his life.

Unlike me. Apparently, I have no fucking say in what happens in my life.

"Hey, man." I pat Coop on the back, taking the stool next to him.

"Hey. Your usual?" he asks me.

"Yep."

He signals to the bartender and orders me a Corona.

"So, what's up?" he asks.

"Everything." *My life. Morgan goddamn Stick-Up-Her-Ass-Ford.*

I drag my hands down my face and let out a groan.

"That bad?"

"Worse," I tell him.

The bartender puts my beer in front of me. I pick it up and down half of the bottle before putting it back down.

"Better?" Coop asks.

"Nope." I slide a look at him. "Mom and Dad went behind my back and hired someone to come and work with me. A 'co-CEO.'" I air-quote.

"Shit. You're kidding."

"Wish I were." I sigh. "And it gets worse. The person they've hired to share my job with me is Morgan Stickford."

"Morgan Stickford…" Coop's brows draw together in thought.

"We went to Northwestern with her," I say. "She always used to sit in the front row. Wore those baggy-ass sweaters all the time. I used to call her Morgan Stick-Up-Her-Ass-Ford."

"Oh, yeah." Coop clicks his fingers in recognition. "Curvy. Blonde hair."

"That's the one."

"Fuck…she hated your guts in college, man." Coop laughs as he picks up his beer and takes a drink. "Why was that?"

"I guess she thought I was a rich prick."

"You are. But so am I. And she didn't hate me."

"Who didn't hate you?" Dom drops into the stool next to Coop.

"Morgan Stickford," Coop tells him. "You remember her from Northwestern?"

"God, yeah. Haven't heard that name in a while though. I used to work shifts with her at Starbucks."

Unlike Coop and me, Dom's family wasn't rich. He was at Northwestern on a scholarship. But he created this dating app after he graduated, and it went big. Really big.

"Did you?" I say to Dom. "How did I not know that?"

Dom shrugs. "She was a nice girl. Didn't like you though, if I remember right."

"She hated his guts," Coop clarifies.

"Thanks for the reminder." I grimace at him.

"I'll have a draft beer," Dom tells the bartender, who just approached. "Why are we talking about Morgan Stickford anyway?" he asks.

"Because Wild's mom and dad just hired her to be the CEO at his company."

"What?" Dom's head swivels to me. "I thought you were getting the job."

"I am. They are bringing her in as co-CEO. Apparently, they think I need a woman's perspective to help me run the company, which is just fucking bullshit and a massive fucking insult."

"Feel for you, man." Dom pats my shoulder and then picks up the beer the bartender just put in front of him.

"What are you gonna do?" Coop asks me.

"Not much I can do." I shrug. "Morgan's coming in tomorrow, and the announcement will be made to the rest of the staff. Then, I have to share my company with her."

God, I fucking hate my life right now.

And I know *hate* is a very strong word, so I won't use it in reference to my parents, but I will say that I seriously, intensely do not like them right now.

"And that's it?" Dom says. "You're just gonna sit back and accept it."

Coop laughs. "Come on, this is Wilder we're talking about. No fucking way will he just roll over and take this. At least, not without a fight."

"Oh, I intend to fight all right." And I'll fight as dirty as I need to. But I need to get my battle plan together, and I can't do that until I meet with Morgan tomorrow and know what her deal is. "But, right now, I'm gonna have a drink with my buddies and maybe shoot some pool later. Who's with me?"

"Always with you, man," Coop says. "But I think we need something stronger than beer for this." He signals the bartender. "Three shots of Jägermeister," he tells him.

"No shots," I tell Coop. "I've got work in the morning."

I can't be hungover when I meet Morgan. Especially not when I have to stand there during the big announcement of her new role in the company.

The thought alone makes me want to puke all over this bar.

"I don't want a shot. I've got an early meeting tomorrow," Dom tells Coop.

"Stop being pussies, the pair of you. Just one shot won't kill you."

"Fine." I sigh. "One shot, and that's it."

"Sure thing, man." Coop grins.

The bartender pours out our drinks. "Enjoy."

Coop picks up a glass and holds it out to us. "Let's toast."

"What the fuck do I have to toast about? How I just lost half of my company?"

"You didn't lose half of your company, dickface." Coop chuckles. "Morgan's just taking half of your job."

"Oh, well, that's okay then," I deadpan.

"Why don't we toast to Wilder finding a way to get rid of Morgan and get his job back?" Dom says.

"He hasn't lost his job though. And wouldn't that be more of a wish?"

"Are you two for real right now?" I stare at them both. "No toasts. And no fucking wishes. Let's just drink, so I can try to forget about this shitty day and the even shittier day that I'm going to have tomorrow." *When Morgan Stickford comes into my office and invades it.*

And, with that horrendous thought in mind, I pick up my shot and throw it back.

J<i>esus Christ.</i>
　　My head is pounding.
　And what the fuck is that noise?
　Is that drilling outside?
　I live on the twenty-first floor, and my windows don't open.
　How the fuck can I hear drilling?
　I lick my dry lips. My mouth feels as dusty as Morgan Stickford's pussy probably was in college.
　Shit. Morgan. She's coming in this morning.
　What time is it?
　I blindly fumble around for my phone on my nightstand. Only there's an empty space where my nightstand usually is.
　I get a sinking feeling right at the same time as I hear a soft groan come from beside me.

Rubbing my eyes before opening them to the muted light in the room, I turn my head, and on the pillow next to me is a mass of long brown hair with a face hidden beneath.

Where the hell am I?

Definitely not a hotel room. There are a selection of bras and panties hanging on the radiator, drying.

Clearly, I got wasted and ended up back at this chick's place.

So much for only one shot. Fucking Cooper.

I need to get out of here and get back to my apartment to get ready to face Morgan.

I slide out of bed, careful not to wake my bed partner up. I can't deal with the morning-after conversation.

I locate my clothes and shoes in a heap on the floor. I pick up my pants and feel my wallet and cell in the pocket.

I pull my cell out and light up the screen.

It's eight thirty.

Shit.

And I have five missed calls from Chrissy and three from my mom, which is odd. But then again, I am usually in the office by now, and they're probably wondering where I am. Especially with Morgan coming in this morning.

I need to get in the office ASAP. I don't have time to go home and change. I'll call Chrissy on the way and ask her to get my clothes ready. I keep a few spare shirts and suits at the office.

I grab my shirt and pull it on, not bothering to button it up, and I slip my sockless feet into my shoes. Fuck knows where my socks are, but I don't have time to look for them. I creep out of her bedroom, through the apartment, and quietly let myself out into the hall.

I look up and down the hallway. I have no fucking clue where the hell I am. The only recollection I have of last night is doing body shots off some chick—I'm assuming the one I just left in bed.

I swear, I'm never drinking again.

Under HER

Ignoring the pounding in my skull, I jog down the hallway and find the stairwell at the end. I'm on the third floor. I run down the stairs, my shirt flapping as I go.

Then, I'm in the empty lobby, and I go out onto the street. Stopping on the sidewalk, I look around.

Where the hell am I? Nothing looks familiar to me right now.

I spy a cab approaching, so I put my hand out to flag it down.

The cab slows at the curbside, and I climb in the back.

"Where to, buddy?"

"Stupid question, but where am I?" I ask the driver.

He chuckles and turns in his seat to look at me. "Rough night?"

"You could say that."

"Well, it must've been a good one if you don't know where you are. You're in Arlington Heights." He taps a finger on the sign on his dash. It reads *Arlington Cabs*. "Where do you need to be?"

"I'm in Arlington Heights? Jesus Christ," I groan.

That's about a forty-five minute drive out of Chicago.

How the hell did I get here?

I drag my hands down my face. "Look, man, I *really* need to be in downtown Chicago—like, about an hour ago."

He gives me an apologetic look. "Sorry, buddy, but I don't take fares out of Arlington."

I lean forward in my seat. "I'll pay you a thousand bucks to take me to Chicago and get me there in the fastest time."

"It's rush hour, man. The quickest I could get you to downtown Chicago would be an hour and a half, and that's if we're lucky. You're looking at more like two hours."

Two hours!

Fuck. My. Life.

"Fine. You get me there in an hour and thirty, and a thousand bucks is yours."

His eyes light up with dollar signs. "You've got yourself a deal," he tells me.

He puts the car in drive, doing a U-turn in the road.

I dial Chrissy. Tucking my cell between my ear and shoulder, I start buttoning up my shirt.

It rings once before she answers.

"Where are you?" she whisper-hisses.

"I'm in a cab, on the way to the office."

"Please tell me you're five minutes away."

"I wish. More like ninety minutes." *If I'm lucky.*

"Ninety minutes!" she screeches.

I wince.

"Where in the world are you?"

"Arlington Heights."

"Arlington Heights! Jesus, Wilder. What are you doing there? Actually, I don't want to know. But your mom is not happy at all. I've been running interference with her. She told me that she called you already, and you didn't answer. Morgan arrived ten minutes ago."

"Shit. She's early." *Kiss-ass.*

"Yeah, well, your mom's not happy because she wanted you to meet with her before the staff meeting, which is happening in an hour."

"An hour!" I slam my hand down on the seat beside me. "The meeting was supposed to be at ten."

"It was brought forward. You got an email about it late last night."

Last night—when I was in a bar, getting trashed and doing body shots off a chick, like I had done back in college.

I'm such a prick.

"Shit." Taking my phone in hand, I lay my head back on the seat and rub my aching forehead. "I'll be there as soon as I can. Just try to delay the meeting until I get there."

"I'll do my best."

I hang up my cell.

I can't fucking believe this. I need to be in Chicago in an hour to make that meeting.

Because, if I don't, I'll never hear the end of it from my mom.

I lean forward in my seat. "Looks like I need to be in Chicago in an hour. I'll add another five hundred to your fare if you get me there."

His eyes meet mine in his rearview mirror. "I'll do my best."

His foot presses down on the gas as I lie back on the seat and pray for a traffic miracle.

5

The cab gets me to the office in an hour and twenty. I pay the driver and jump out of the cab like my ass is on fire. I race my way into the building and straight into a waiting elevator.

I jab at the button to my floor, impatiently watching the door close. Then, finally, it starts to ascend.

I tuck my shirt into my pants, and staring at my blurred reflection on the shiny metal walls of the elevator, I run my hands through my hair, trying to straighten it.

The elevator reaches my floor. The door opens, and Chrissy is waiting there with a coffee in hand.

"You look like shit."

"Thanks." I take the coffee from her, and we start walking side by side in the direction of my office. "Has the meeting started yet?"

"No. Your parents pushed it back."

"My mom pissed?"

Chrissy slides me a look. "What do you think?"

I think I'm dead.

"They're waiting for you in your office with Morgan."

"Okay." I take a gulp of coffee.

"And your parents think that a pipe burst at your apartment and that you had to get the plumbers in, so that's why you're late."

"You're the best," I tell her.

"Oh, I know." She smirks.

My stomach growls loudly. I realize I haven't eaten since lunch yesterday. No wonder I got so hammered last night.

"You hungry?"

"Apparently so."

"I think there are some muffins and brownies in the conference room, but I'll put an order in for waffles at your usual place."

Waffles. Best pick-me-up food ever.

"Thanks, Chrissy. Honestly, I don't know what I'd do without you."

"You'd crash and burn. But, luckily for you, that will never happen 'cause I'm here to stay."

"You're due a pay raise soon, right?"

"Yep." She grins.

We reach my office door. I take another drink of my coffee and hand it off to Chrissy.

She gives me an encouraging smile. "You've got this."

I take a deep breath and pull my shoulders back. Then, I push open my door and walk in my office.

I hear Chrissy make a noise behind me, like a gasp, but I ignore her and stride confidently into my office.

"Mom, Dad." I smile at them. "So sorry I'm late."

My mom returns my smile, but I can see she's pissed at me. The tightening around her mouth gives it away. I've seen that mouth tighten a lot over the years.

My dad greets me, coming over to pat my back. "Don't worry, son. It's not your fault you had plumbing problems."

If I'd had plumbing problems, then I wouldn't have been so late. I swallow down.

"Wilder, you remember Morgan." My mom gestures to my sofa.

For the first time in nine years, my eyes take in Morgan Stickford.

And, holy fuck, she's changed.

"Yes, of course." I walk forward to greet her, my eyes fixed on her.

She rises to her feet, her lips pressing into a smile. I think it's the first time I've ever seen her smile in my direction. I used to get a sneer, and that was on a good day.

Dad makes a strangled noise behind me, but I'm too busy taking in Morgan to pay him any mind.

Because hello, hottie.

Morgan Stickford is all grown-up. And she's a full-fledged babe.

She was pretty in college. But, now, she's a fucking knockout. She's thinner than she used to be, but she's still rocking those curves in all the right places.

She's wearing a pale pink pencil dress that has a slit up the front, finishing mid thigh, showing enough of her gorgeous tan legs to tease. The dress hugs her body, showcasing her amazing figure.

Jesus, her body is smoking.

She looks the same but different. Still fresh-faced. But, now, she wears a little more makeup than she used to in college. Pouty lips painted pink. Wide brown eyes lined with thick black lashes, staring back at me, not giving anything away, but they look a hell of a lot warmer than they used to look at me back in college. Her long, straight honey-blonde hair is down, falling around her shoulders.

She's stunning.

She looks like she should be modeling our product, not selling it.

"It's great to see you again," I say. And it really fucking is.

Her smile widens, showing a slip of her white teeth. Then, she parts her lips to speak—hopefully to say, *Please fuck me, Wilder*, although that's not likely, as my parents are here—when my mom's voice slices through the air.

"Wilder! What is on the back of your shirt?"

I stop at the shrill tone of my mom's voice, my eyes jerking in her direction. "What?" I ask, confused.

"Your shirt!" Mom starts to advance on me, clear anger in her eyes.

My shirt? What the hell is she talking about?

Before my mom can reach me, I turn to look at myself in the wall mirror on the other side of my office. As I move, I see Chrissy's wide eyes, her lips pressed tightly together. I catch sight of my dad, and his fist is pressed to his lips. He's clearly fighting laughter.

What the fuck is going on?

Then, I hear Morgan gasp. I swing my eyes back to hers, and the warmth that was in them has been replaced with barely concealed disgust.

What the hell is happening here right now?

Pulling my eyes from Morgan, I turn my back to the mirror, looking at it over my shoulder, trying to see what everyone else is seeing, and—

No. That can't be. Surely not.

I squint my eyes, trying to take in what I'm seeing. I back up, so I'm closer to the mirror, my eyes glued to it, and all too soon, it becomes clear.

"What the hell?" I hiss.

How did that get there?

Well, I have a pretty good idea how it got there. I just don't know *when* it was put there. Or why the fuck someone would do that.

How the hell did I not see this when I was getting dressed?

Under
HER

I know I was bleary-eyed, and the room was semidark, but it's not like you can frigging miss it.

Because written there, on the back of my light-gray shirt, in clear black ink is…

Last night was incredible! You really are Wild. ;)

Call me if you want to fuck again.

847-206-7841

xoxo

Holy. Frigging. Hell.

6

Morgan
Thirteen Years Ago

Sitting in my seat in the front row of the lecture hall, I try to listen as Professor George starts to talk, but my neck is sore and aching. I roll my head, hand pressed to the back of my neck, trying to ease the pressure.

It doesn't work.

My neck is stiff because I spent the night on the floor of my best friend, Joely's, dorm room—and not by choice.

Joely and I had gone to high school together, and we'd decided to come to Northwestern together. We'd agreed that we'd room separately, so we could meet new people.

Joely had gotten an awesome roommate—Hannah.

I'd gotten the roommate from hell—Tori.

And I had to crash on Joely and Hannah's floor because Tori had locked me out of our room.

The thought alone makes me grind my teeth in anger, and I ignore the ache in my chest when I recall the reason she'd locked me out of our room.

Wilder Cross.

The guy I stupidly have a crush on. Not that he even knows my name. A girl like me doesn't register on the radar of a guy like Wilder.

He's ridiculously beautiful with a head full of dirty-blond hair and bright blue eyes, the kind that you just want to fall into, and along with all of that is a tall, muscular body that tells me he visits the gym often. He's the full package.

He's part of Northwestern's elite. The rich, beautiful crowd.

And he spent last night in my dorm room, screwing my roommate.

It makes sense that he would go for someone like Tori. She might be a bitch, but she's gorgeous. Thin, big boobs, long, dark hair, and olive skin. She looks like she just stepped out of a L'Oréal commercial. And she comes from a wealthy family. Her dad's the head of some bank or something.

She's Wilder's kind.

I, on the other hand, come from a working-class family. My dad is an electrician, and my mom is a beautician. I'm here at Northwestern on a scholarship. I've always been too focused on schoolwork to care about boys, but the moment I saw Wilder, there was just something about him. Something I liked.

Until last night, that is.

Of course, I've heard the gossip—that Wilder is a player and a self-righteous prick—but I've always chosen not to listen to rumors.

Under
HER

My mom has always said that what people project isn't necessarily a true reflection of themselves. She says most people will only ever show you what they want you to know, and if you want to know more, then it's up to you to dig a little deeper and get to know them properly. So, I never make snap judgments about people.

Maybe that should change.

Because I was clearly wrong about Wilder. Not that I had known much about him before last night. But, in the little I'd gleamed from him in my time at Northwestern, I'd thought he seemed nice. He was always smiling and joking around with his friends. And I'd figured, even if he was a man-whore, it didn't make him a bad person, so long as he was up-front with the girls he was man-whoring with.

But I was wrong.

Wilder isn't a nice guy.

He's an asshole in the first degree.

Late last night after a long-ass shift at Starbucks, I was tired, and all I wanted to do was fall facedown on my bed and sleep. But, when I got home, I couldn't get in my room. The door was locked, and my key wouldn't turn, like the lock had been jammed from the other side.

Stupidly, I had a flash of worry for Tori—until I heard a load moan come from behind the door and the sound of Tori giggling. That was when I realized that Tori had locked me out of our room. It wasn't the first time she'd pulled this kind of shit on me. So, I saw red. I hammered on the door, and when Tori finally opened up, wearing only her bra and panties, she had a scowl on her face, her dark hair all tousled up.

Then, I saw Wilder lying on her bed, naked, except for his boxer shorts.

And I wanted to throw up.

"What?" Tori snapped, like I had no right to even be knocking on our door.

I blinked at her in surprise. "Um, I'm really tired, Tori. I've had a long day, and I really just want to go to sleep."

"So?" Her hand went to her hip.

"So, can you find somewhere else to…" I gestured a hand in the direction of Wilder without looking at him. I wasn't going to say the words, and I definitely wasn't going to look at him again.

"No," she said.

"No?" I echoed in surprise.

"No. I'm busy, and we're going to be busy all night, so you'll have to find somewhere else to sleep tonight."

While she was saying that, Wilder had gotten up from her bed, and he came up behind her, sliding his hands around her waist and kissing her neck.

All I could do was stare at them. Angry at what she'd said and crushed, watching him touch her like that.

Then, his eyes lifted, and he looked straight at me. His eyes were glazed from alcohol. "Let her in," he said to Tori but not taking his eyes off me. "She can watch. Maybe even join in. She looks like she could do with some loosening up."

I heard a strangled noise, and when Wilder smirked, I realized that it had come from me.

Embarrassment stung my cheeks. I curled my hand into the hem of my work shirt.

"You ass!" Tori slapped his arm as she turned in to face him. "Aren't I enough for you?" She pouted.

"Course you are, babe." Wilder let an arm drop from around her and shut the door in my face.

I was too flabbergasted to react.

Then, I heard Tori say from behind the door, "You didn't mean that, did you? About her joining in?"

He chuckled, deep and low. "Course not. I was just fucking around."

"Good, because I didn't think Wilder Cross was into fat chicks."

Under HER

Fat? I'm not fat!

Okay, sure, I had curves, and I was a size eight or ten, depending on the store, but that wasn't exactly fat.

Is it?

He laughed, and that hurt more than her fat comment. Because his laughter only confirmed that he agreed with her.

And it was proven when he said, "You know me, babe. Anything over a size four, and I show her the door."

I sucked in a painful breath as I staggered away.

I didn't want to hear any more. I'd heard enough.

He thinks I'm...fat.

I'd never been called fat before. I knew I wasn't super skinny, but fat never came into the equation.

I glanced down at my body, suddenly seeing myself through their eyes...*his* eyes.

Tears started to blur my vision, and I swiped a hand over my eyes. I hated them both in that moment...and myself for letting them get to me like that.

And for having a crush on such an asshole.

An asshole who only cared about the physical size of a girl and had no qualms over kicking me out of my room with no regard for where I would be sleeping tonight just so he could get laid.

Those two things told me everything I needed to know about Wilder Cross.

The bang of the door in the lecture hall brings my eyes to it, as it does everyone else in here.

It's Wilder, arriving late for our lecture. His arm is slung around the shoulders of a girl who's not Tori. Honestly, I'm not sure if I've ever seen her in this lecture before. He probably just picked her up outside.

She's definitely under a size four, so I guess she won't be shown the door.

Meow. Saucer of milk needed in the front row for yours truly.

I will not let Wilder's idiot comment from last night bother me. I don't care what he thinks about me.

Only that's a lie, and I do care.

Wilder strides through the lecture hall, heading for the seats, with his minus-four companion in tow. Neither of them apologizes to our professor for their tardiness.

Assholes.

But, even still, my eyes track him without my permission.

Without warning, he looks straight over at me, like he felt me staring at him.

Heat rises in my cheeks, but I don't look away. I let all my anger into my eyes.

I want him to know that I'm pissed at him for last night.

I see a whisper of confusion cross his brow, like he can't figure out why I'm annoyed with him.

The fact that he can't remember annoys me even more. The moment—no, *I* was so insignificant for him that he can't even remember.

My hands curl into fists, and my pulse starts to throb in my neck.

I want him to remember. And I want him to feel bad.

I watch in those seconds that feel like hours, hoping for a hint of an apology in his eyes. Hell, I'd even take guilt.

But I get neither.

I get something, but honestly, I'd rather have had his ignorance.

Because do you know what the bastard does?

He smirks and winks at me.

My heart falls into the pit of my stomach, and hurt and embarrassment fill me.

And that is the exact moment that I stop crushing on Wilder Cross and start hating on him instead.

The meeting finished half an hour ago. I was dressed in a clean shirt and suit. Thank God I keep spares in my office. Never thought I'd need them for that reason though.

The announcement about Morgan and me was made, and Morgan stood up to introduce herself to everyone. I'm pretty sure she told everyone where she was from and regaled her previous job history to them along with what she hoped to achieve here, but I didn't absorb a word because, honestly, I was stuck in my head, silently fuming over the shirt incident.

I swear, it's like someone has it out for me.

I mean, who in the hell writes a note about how great the sex was? Granted, it was great because, hello, this is me we're talking about. But, writing that and her phone number on the back of my shirt, it's just crazy behavior.

Whatever happened to just slipping a guy your number on a piece of paper? Is writing on the guy's clothes a new thing? I hope to fuck not. Thank God I won't be seeing that chick again.

I could really have done without that happening the first time I saw Morgan after all these years.

She looked at me like I was the same piece of shit that she'd thought I was in college, and I can't blame her.

I didn't get a chance to explain, not that my explanation would have had me coming off sounding great, because my mom ushered her out of the office, leaving me with Chrissy and my dad, who thought it was highly fucking amusing. I bet he won't be laughing about it to my mom though.

I know for sure that I'm in for a lecture from my mom.

Aside from the side-eyed stares she kept giving me during the meeting, I was treated to *the look* right before she and Dad left to go to their meeting with their broker.

But I'll deal with Mom later.

Right now, I need to speak to Morgan.

I wanted to talk to her after the meeting was done, but I couldn't get her alone for a second. Then, I had to take a business call on my cell, so I stepped out of the conference room, and when I came back, she was gone. I asked Chrissy if she knew where Morgan was, and Chrissy told me she was up in her new office, checking it out.

So, here I am, on my way to her office. Tail between my legs. Figuratively. Because my actual tail is very keen on getting between *her* legs.

But that's never going to happen.

A: Because she probably still thinks I'm the same prick that she thought I was nine years ago.

And B: We work together now. She might be on my level managerially, but ultimately, this company is going to be mine one day, so in an indirect way, that makes her an employee.

The door to Morgan's office is open when I approach. She's got her back to me, staring out the window.

Her office used to belong to Dennis Walsh. He was Deputy CEO. He died suddenly a year and a half ago of a heart attack. My parents never refilled his position, and his office has stood empty ever since. They just distributed his work between themselves and me. He'd worked for them forever, and he'd been a good friend to them, so it hit them hard, losing him. It hit us all hard.

So, it's a little weird to see Morgan standing in here, in his office. I half-expect to hear the sound of Dennis's big, booming laughter.

The office is bare, except for Dennis's old desk and chair.

She'll need new furniture.

"You like the view?" I say in a soft voice so as not to startle her.

I see her back stiffen at the sound of my voice, which isn't a good sign, and then she looks at me over her shoulder before turning to face me.

"It's stunning."

So are you. The thought pops into my head out of nowhere.

But I'm right. She is stunning.

"You're going to need new furniture." I gesture to the sparse space.

Her eyes move around. "Yeah."

"I'll get my PA, Chrissy, to email you the link to the website of the office supplier we use. Just pick out what you need and let Chrissy know, and she'll have it here for you when you start on Monday."

"That'll be great. Thanks."

There's a brief lull of silence between us.

"Has my mom mentioned anything about hiring a PA for you?" I ask her.

She nods. "Yes. Your mom lined up some interviews for me, so I should be sorted soon."

"Good...great."

We slip into that goddamn silence again.

I just need to say what I came here to say and then get out of here.

"Look, Morgan…" I rub a hand over my hair. "What happened earlier in my office…what you saw on the back of my shirt—"

"Is none of my business," she cuts me off.

"I know, but I just want you to know that's not the norm for me. I'm never usually late or unprofessional in that way. It was just…" I can't exactly tell her that I was out, drinking at a bar, because I was freaking out over her starting work here and taking half of my job.

"Honestly, you don't have to explain, Wilder."

The way she says my name, it's like hearing it for the first time. Sure, she must've said my name to me in college, but it never felt like this. Like a cattle prod to the spine, sparking my dick to life. Well, not that he seems to be asleep in her presence, but you know what I mean. Seriously though, I would have for sure remembered if hearing her say my name back in college made me feel that way. I'd have found a way to get her to like me, so I could have screwed her. Shallow bastard that I am.

"I think I do." I take a breath. "I know that we didn't get along great in college—"

"Didn't we?" She tilts her head. The amusement dancing in her eyes surprises me.

I let loose a smile on my lips. "Come on, Morgan, we both know I wasn't your favorite person back then, and you didn't exactly make that fact unknown to me."

She laughs, and the sound runs through my veins like alcohol in my bloodstream.

"Okay," she concedes, "I didn't like you. But you didn't like me either."

I cock my head. "I liked you just fine—well, in the beginning until you incorrectly decided that I was an overprivileged prick and started hating on me."

The humor fades from her eyes, and I know I said the wrong thing and took us back a step.

She presses her lips together, like she's holding back from saying something, and before whatever words she's fighting back can get out, I jump in.

"Look, this isn't coming out right." I rub a hand over my face. "What I'm trying to say is, whatever happened back then or what we thought of each other doesn't matter. We're different people now. College was forever ago. Neither of us knows the 2017 versions of each other, and I would really like for us to wipe the slate clean and start fresh from here."

"When you say 'wipe the slate clean,' do you mean, forget the sex note on the back of your shirt, too?"

"Jesus." I shake my head. "I'm never gonna live that down, am I?"

Her lips twitch, like she's fighting a smile. "Probably not."

"In all seriousness, I just want you to know that's the first time anything like that has ever happened to me. It was just one of those screwup kind of days that happened on the worst day."

Her brows knit together. "Me starting today is your worst day?"

"No!" *Yes. Kind of.* "No, I mean—"

"Wilder."

"What?"

"I'm messing with you." She smiles.

"Oh. Right. Okay." I jam my hands in my pants pockets. "Well, anyway, I just want you to know that I am sorry for what happened before, and I do always keep my personal life away from work. I'm all business when I'm here."

"Me, too," she says.

"That's good then—that we're on the same page." I free my hands from my pockets and walk toward her. My heart rate picks up, the closer I get to her.

She smells feminine, floral and sweet. Like a bouquet of flowers. I want to bury my head in her neck and taste that scent on the tip of my tongue.

I put my hand out to her. "Clean slate," I say, staring straight into her big doe eyes.

She blinks once and then glances down at my hand before looking back up to meet me. She slips her hand into mine. Her hand is soft, and I'm desperately trying not to wonder how that hand would feel around my cock.

"Hi, clean slate. I'm Morgan Stickford."

"Wilder Cross." I grin and shake her hand, thinking that Morgan working here might not be the worst thing in the world after all.

It's Friday afternoon, and I'm knee deep in work when there's a tap at my door.

I look up from my computer screen to see Morgan standing in my office doorway. She's looking exceptionally, torturously gorgeous in a black pencil skirt with a deep red silk shirt tucked into it, showing off her tiny waist and her more-than-a-handful rack. To top off my torment, her lips are painted the same shade as her shirt, and she's wearing black come-fuck-me heels on her feet. Her hair is pinned up, begging for me to free it and run my fingers through it while I fuck her senseless over my desk.

Jesus. I really need to get laid.

And I really need to stop thinking of her in a sexual way.

"Hey." I smile. "You okay?"

"Yeah. Sorry to interrupt. Your mom said you have the file on Buxom. I was hoping to take it home this weekend, so I can become familiar with them."

Buxom is one of our largest distributors.

We have stores across the country, but we also have in-store distributors in cities where we don't have a physical store.

She chews on her lip, like she's nervous for some reason, and it's doing no good for my self-control.

No sex with coworkers. No sex with coworkers.

I clearly need to keep repeating that to myself when I'm around Morgan, as my dick doesn't seem to be getting the message.

"Sure." I get up from my chair and go to get the file off the shelf. I walk over to her and hand her the file.

"Thanks," she says, holding it to her chest.

She's still lingering in my doorway, so I lean back against my desk to face her.

"How's your first week been?" I ask her.

"Really great." She gives me a smile, flashing me those straight white teeth of hers.

"My mom's not overloading you with information, is she? She's awesome, but she has a tendency to forget that not everyone knows as much about this company as she does."

"No, she's been great. I like her a lot. And your dad, too."

"Yeah, they're both pretty awesome."

"Must feel strange for you—them retiring. After working here with them for so long."

"Yeah, it'll be strange, but I'm looking forward to the challenge of running this company. With your help, of course," I add.

"Of course." Her lips quirk at the corner. She leans her shoulder against the doorframe. "Look, I heard something today, and I don't know if it's just office gossip, but I wanted to check. You were originally supposed to run the company yourself, and then your parents recruited me to work with you, as they felt you needed a female counterbalance, but they didn't tell you until I was actually hired."

Irritation flashes through me. I cross a leg over my other and fold my arms as I take a breath. "That's pretty much it, yeah."

Her shoulders sag a little. "Okay, well, I just wanted you to know that I didn't know. I mean, your parents didn't keep anything from me when they offered me the job. I knew I'd be working with you, but I wasn't aware that you didn't know."

"You knew you'd be working with me, yet you still took the job?" I lilt my voice, so she knows I'm teasing, and honestly, I'm ready to move the conversation away from the subject. It's still a sore one with me.

"Shocker, huh?" She widens her eyes. "But, honestly, the pay package and benefits were way too good to refuse."

That makes me chuckle. "You were at Oscars before here. Managing Director of Marketing, right?"

Oscars is a female clothing company.

"Yeah."

"You've done well for yourself since college."

She shrugs, as if dismissing my words. "So have you."

I don't know if that's a dig or not, so I choose to go with the latter, and I'm right to do so because she follows it with, "I heard that you went to Columbia after Northwestern. Then, you started here, in the bottom ranks, and worked your way up to where you are now."

"Who told you that?"

"Your mom." She smiles. "She also said that you probably had it harder than any employee here, as you felt you had to prove that you'd earned everything and you weren't just given it."

It's my turn to give a shrug. "Sounds like my mom's been bragging about me."

"She's proud of you."

It's nice to hear that. I know my parents are proud of me, but hearing it never grows old.

There's a lull between us. But it's not the awkward lull that we had last week when I went to her office. And, this time, we're looking at each other. Neither looking away. And this silence is definitely filled with something...

"So, I should..." She thumbs over her shoulder, not finishing her sentence.

"Yeah." I clear my throat. "I really need to get on with this; otherwise, I'll be here all night." I round my desk and sit down in my chair.

"Thanks for this." She lifts the folder away from her chest before clasping it back to her, and for a moment, I'm jealous of that folder, all squished up against her tits.

As she turns away, I feel the weird urge to keep her here even if for just one more moment.

"Did you manage to get a PA sorted?" I ask her.

She stops and turns back to me. "Yeah." She smiles. "I interviewed three candidates yesterday, and there was one who was a standout—Sierra. I called her up earlier to offer her the position, and she accepted. Great thing is, she can start on Monday, as she'd been temping and her temp job finished last week."

"That's great, Morgan. I hope she's as good a PA for you as Chrissy is for me."

Seriously, there's nothing more valuable than a great PA. Chrissy is like gold dust. Great PAs are hard to come by. If Chrissy ever decided to leave me, I wouldn't be too proud to get on my knees and beg her to stay.

"Answer wisely, Morgan." Chrissy's voice carries through to my office from her desk outside.

Morgan chuckles and glances over her shoulder, out of my office and at Chrissy. "I don't think it's possible to find a better PA than you," Morgan says to her.

Then, she looks back at me, bites the corner of her painted lip, and winks. It's the hottest thing I've ever seen.

Under
HER

She is the hottest thing I've ever seen.

And I've seen a lot of hot.

My cock hardens instantly, like an iron spike in my pants, and I thank the fucking Lord that I'm sitting down and that my desk is hiding my preteen dick.

"Thanks again for this." Morgan taps the folder with her fingers. "Have a great weekend. I'll see you on Monday."

"Yeah," I mutter because I'm still in shock.

I just got hard, and I'm talking a full-on raging boner that's still here from Morgan biting her lip and winking at me.

That hasn't happened to me in…well, ever.

And I haven't had a random, inappropriate hard-on since I was a teenager when they were par for the course.

Seriously, what the fuck is going on?

I'm not one of those guys who is all about the forbidden fruit and the chase. I'm not the kind of guy who wants something purely because he can't have it.

I don't have to go after the unobtainable because there's more than enough of the obtainable out there for me.

In the past, there have been women who worked here, some seriously hot women, who I would have happily screwed, but it never bothered me that I couldn't, and I definitely didn't sprout random erections because of a lip bite and wink from them.

I just don't understand what's going on with me at the moment.

It's stress. It has to be.

I've had a lot going on this past week.

Or maybe… after all these years, I have actually grown tired of all the easy pussy, and the fact that I can't have Morgan is doing these crazy things to my cock. And she did used to hate me in college, so there's the added challenge.

Yeah, that's it.

It has to be. There's no other explanation for it.

So, all I need to do is ignore this stupid forbidden-fruit infatuation that my cock has with Morgan until it passes. And, in the meantime, I'll screw as much pussy as possible to keep my dick occupied on other things and not her.

I left the office late on Friday, as my work had taken me twice as long because my mind kept drifting to thoughts of Morgan and all the sex I wanted to have with her.

I'm a guy. Of course I think of sex on the regular. Not every seven seconds, as theorists suggest, but definitely a lot.

I fucking love sex. What's not to love about screwing a hot woman until you're both hot and sweaty and coming hard?

But, after Morgan left my office, all I could think of was her. How hard she made me from one look. And I was fast heading toward breaking the every-seven-seconds theory. I couldn't get thoughts of her out of my head. Her bent over my desk while I fucked her from behind. Then, on my desk. On my sofa. Up against the wall. Her on her knees, sucking my cock. Me on my knees, licking her pussy. Then, in the shower of my private bathroom, fucking under the hot spray. I even veered off to thoughts of screwing her on my bed at home. That was when I knew shit was getting crazy.

I stopped off in the diner near my apartment building to grab a takeout burger. The waitress who served me was hot. Not Morgan hot, but hot.

She slipped me her number as she handed me the burger.

I wasn't going to call her. But then I got home, and while I ate my burger and drank a beer, the Morgan-sex-scenario reel in my brain started playing again, and my dick was aching from all the teasing my brain had been doing.

So, I called the takeout girl and went to her place after her shift ended.

What? Don't judge me. I'm a guy, and I needed to have sex. I needed the release.

Only it didn't make me feel as good as I had been hoping it would. My balls still felt blue even though I'd just come, and I had this weird feeling in my chest. If I didn't know better, I might say it was…guilt.

Which was weird because I had nothing to feel guilty about.

Afterward, I went back to my apartment and lay awake, thinking about—yep, you got it—sex and Morgan. Or sex with Morgan.

I figured I'd be okay by Saturday night. Once I was out with the boys, I'd be back to normal.

Yeppers, you guessed it. I was wrong.

I wasn't feeling it. Or any chick in the bar. So, for the first time in a really long time, I went home alone on a Saturday night.

I skipped brunch with the guys, feigning illness, as I didn't feel like listening to their sexual proclivities from the night before or admitting that I hadn't had one of my own to share.

I honestly don't know what the hell is going on with me.

It must be a blip. Maybe I'm having some kind of early-thirties crisis.

I figure I just need to avoid seeing Morgan as much as possible, which is hard, considering I have to work with her. But, if I keep her at arm's and eye's length, then my cock will get over this little obsession that he has with her, and things will go back to normal.

It's Tuesday morning, and I'm heading into the office. I wasn't in yesterday, as I was in Kentucky all day, meeting with our supplier of satin knit, which we use to make our panties.

I say, "Good morning," to Leah, ignoring her come-fuck-me eyes. I've got enough going on with my internal battle without having to contend with her.

I head straight to the elevators and press the call button, waiting.

The elevator door opens. When I'm inside, I hear the click of heels on the tiled floor.

Please don't be Morgan.

I really don't want to be stuck in a small space with her while my cock is acting up like it has been.

But it's not Morgan. It's a brunette who I don't recognize.

I should be relieved that it's not Morgan, but I'm not because a tiny, sadistic part of me was actually hoping that it was Morgan.

"Which floor?" I ask the brunette.

I slide a look at her. She's cute. But I don't know her, and I know everyone who works here. Maybe she's here for an early meeting with one of the teams.

"Fourteen."

That's my floor. My brows come together in confusion as I reach out to push the button. Then, it dawns on me. She must be Morgan's new PA.

"Your Morgan's new PA," I say as the door closes.

I dip my chin to look at her and find that she's already staring up at me.

I feel a jolt of familiarity.

"I did wonder if it was you when Morgan told me the name of the CEO. Wilder's not a name you hear often. And it is you. Clearly, you don't remember me."

Her green eyes flash with something, and she tips her chin up and takes a step closer.

Fuck. Fuck. Fuck.

She knows me. And I have a sinking feeling I know exactly how she knows me. Because I've had sex with her. Most women only know me for that reason.

But I don't remember her. Not even a flicker.

Have I screwed that many women that I no longer remember them?

Honestly, I think I already know the answer to that question because it's standing right in front of me.

I'm starting to sweat. "Of course I remember you." I swallow roughly against the lie.

She laughs. It tinkles in the small space, which feels like it's getting smaller by the second.

"Wow. Was I that forgettable?" Hurt flashes through her eyes. "It was less than a week ago when you were in my bed, screwing me senseless. But I guess it makes sense that you didn't call me if you'd forgotten me the moment you left my place. I'm guessing that's why you snuck out while I was still sleeping."

Less than a week ago? The only women I've had sex with this past week were the waitress from Friday—and she's definitely not her because she was a redhead and a true one, as the carpet matched the drapes—and this chick…

Under HER

Oh, fuck no.
Arlington Heights. The shirt-writer.

"Arlington Heights," I blurt out, feeling a shot of familiarity, the more I stare at her face. "You wrote on my shirt."

"That's me. And my name is Sierra," she says in a haughty voice. She folds her arms over her chest. "I'm the girl from Arlington Heights who you hooked up with last week and never called."

"And you're…" I can't bring myself to say the words.

"Morgan's PA," she finishes for me.

Oh, fucking no. Just fucking no.

The elevator pings its arrival, and the door opens, but I can't stop staring at Sierra. The shirt-writer from Arlington.

It's like the worst kind of joke. It'd be funny if it wasn't so goddamn bad.

"Oh, hey!" The chipper tone in Morgan's voice makes me nearly shit my pants. "You two have already met."

I turn my head to look at Morgan standing there, outside the elevator, smiling and looking sexy as hell, and my dick shrivels up and dies in my pants.

Well, I wanted him to quit getting hard around her. I guess screwing her new PA has done that.

Granted, I didn't know she was going to be Morgan's PA when I fucked her. But I somehow don't think Morgan would see it that way.

"Yes, we've already met," Sierra says in a sweet tone. But there's nothing sweet about the look in her eyes as she walks past me and out of the elevator. She looks like she either wants to punch me in the mouth or kiss the shit out of it. Either way, it's not good.

Shit. Fucking. Shit.

"You staying in there?" Morgan chuckles, bringing my eyes to hers.

"No."

I step out, and she gets in the elevator.

"Oh, Wilder, can we chat later? I've got an idea that I want to run by you."

"Sure. I'm here all day," I say. My mouth is dry. I feel like I'm talking through cotton wool.

"Great. I'll call Chrissy and have her schedule me in." She reaches over and pushes the elevator button.

My eyes move to the retreating figure of Sierra going through the door to the executive offices.

I hold back the sigh I feel.

"Hey." The sound of Morgan's soft voice pulls me back. She's watching me, a little furrow in her brows, her head tilted to the side. "You okay?"

Well, let's see. The chick I screwed last week after I got hammered because I was pissed about you coming to work here—thus being the reason I was late to our meeting, where I found she'd also left me a sex note on the back of my shirt—is now working here, for you. That kind of puts a kink in my strict rule of never sleeping with employees. And, also, I have this maddening urge to fuck you on every surface of my office and home until neither of us can walk straight.

So, to answer your question, no, I'm not okay.

"Yep." I smile wide. "I'm great. I'll see you later." I turn and speed walk in the direction of my office.

Chrissy isn't at her desk when I get there, and for once, I'm relieved not to see her, as conversation isn't something I'm up for at the moment.

I get into the safety of my office, close the door, and lean back against it. I cover my face with my hands and let out a groan.

Fuck my life.

What are the odds? First, Morgan, the girl who hated my guts in college, comes here and takes half of my job. And, now, one of my recent one-night stands is here, working for her.

I swear to God, you couldn't write this shit.

If I were a superstitious person, then I would seriously be thinking that the universe had it out for me.

I spend the rest of the day hiding out in my office.

I'm a pussy. I know.

But I just don't want to run into Sierra. Or Morgan. Or my mother.

That woman is like a sniffer dog when it comes to knowing there's an issue with me.

She's still not fully forgiven me for the whole shirt incident, so I definitely don't want her knowing that it was Sierra's handiwork.

Morgan wanted to see me, and when she called to schedule a meeting, I had Chrissy tell her something had come up and that I couldn't see her until tomorrow.

Chrissy raised a brow when I told her to blow Morgan off until tomorrow, but she never questioned my motives.

It was a shitty thing to do, but I just don't want to face her right now.

I'm all confused about wanting to fuck her. Okay, so I'm not confused about actually wanting to fuck her. I'm perplexed about *how* much I want to fuck her and also the fact that I have a feeling, even if I did have her, once wouldn't be enough.

And, also, I need time to figure out how to handle the Sierra problem.

I could be overreacting; maybe there won't be a problem at all.

Oh, who am I kidding? There'll definitely be an issue. I saw the look in Sierra's eyes as she left the elevator. In her mind, I'd run out on her while she slept, and I apparently never called her.

Not like I'd said I was going to. I'm pretty sure I'd had *the talk* with her—the one where I tell the women that I'm not in it for anything more than that night. Even though I had been hammered, the talk is as essential as wearing a condom. But, as I can hardly remember anything about that night, I can't be a hundred percent sure of it.

And I know women, especially pissed off women, and Sierra's definitely pissed at me.

I just don't know to what level of pissed-off-ness.

I need to carefully handle her; otherwise, she could cause me a headache at work—namely, with my mom and Morgan—and I could really do without that.

My focus needs to be on being the best CEO, but all my time at the moment seems to be swallowed up with women.

When did my life become so complicated?

Oh, yeah, the day Morgan Stickford came back into it.

I decide to leave work early. I need to clear my head and let off some steam, so I arrange to meet Coop in Ada Park to shoot some hoops.

I fucking love it there. Coop and I have been going there to play ball since we were kids. Dom is still at work, as I should be, but he's going to meet us for a drink later—a nonalcoholic drink. It was drinking during the week that got me into the mess I'm currently in.

I'm at the court before Coop, so I set my bag and water bottle down on the courtside and start shooting some hoops on my own.

I start dribbling the ball, and then I stop, turn, and shoot. The ball goes through the net.

I jog over and retrieve it, continuing to shoot hoops, while I wait for Coop to arrive.

I wipe my forehead with my hand. I'm starting to sweat already, and I've barely gotten started. It is warm though. I'm thankful that I changed into gym shorts and a wifebeater before leaving the office. Not that I'd ever play ball in my suit.

I line up to take another shot when the sound of Coop's voice behind me stops me. "Fifty bucks says you miss."

I glance at him over my shoulder. "Hundred, and you're on."

Coop drops his bag to the floor and nods, accepting the bet.

I take the shot, and it goes in.

"Lucky fucker." Coop chuckles.

"Skilled fucker, you mean." I laugh. "You should know never to bet against me on hoops, Coop. I never miss." I walk over and get the ball, tossing it to Coop. "Double or nothing that you miss."

Coop flips me off. "Say good-bye to your Franklins."

He takes the shot, and the ball hits the hoop and bounces off.

I laugh.

"Fuck off," Cooper says. "There's something wrong with this ball."

"Yeah, you keep telling yourself that, man."

I catch the ball as he tosses it to me, and without pause, I shoot, and it goes straight through. "What were you saying about the ball?"

"You're a dick," he grunts.

I laugh as I get the ball and hand it over to Coop.

"So, what's up?" he asks me as he lines up his next shot.

"What makes you think anything's up?"

"It's Tuesday afternoon, and you're here with me, shooting hoops. You're usually chained to your office desk at this time. It doesn't take a genius to figure out that something's wrong. I'm gonna go with…Morgan." He takes a shot and misses.

"Kind of." I sigh. I go get the ball and pass it back to him to try again.

"I thought things were going okay with her. You said she was cool."

"She is cool." I pause and look at him. "But she might not be when she finds out that I boned her new assistant."

His wide eyes dart to mine, and he laughs. "You didn't."

"I did. And it's not funny, man."

"It kinda is." He takes a shot, and it goes in. "What happened to your no-screwing-at-work rule? She must be hot as hell to get you to break that."

I go over to retrieve the ball. "I didn't break the rule—technically. You know the chick I banged last week, the one who wrote on my shirt? Well, it's her. Morgan hired her to be her new PA."

"Holy shit." He laughs again, louder this time. "All of the women in Chicago, and she hires her."

"I know, right? And, now, I don't know what to do. Should I tell Morgan or not?" I lift the ball in my hands, line up, and throw. The ball goes through the hoop.

"She's not your girlfriend, dude," Coop says as he goes and gets the ball. "You just work together. What you do in your private life is your business…unless…"

His brows go up, and I know what he's thinking. He's thinking I banged Morgan.

"Jesus, man," I tell him. "I haven't touched Morgan, and I'm not going to." *But, fuck, I want to.*

"Why not? You said she was hot."

"She is, but I work with her. And, now, her PA is an ex-conquest. It just makes things awkward."

"Only if you let it. You don't plan on banging this chick…"

"Sierra."

"You don't plan on banging Sierra again?"

"Definitely not."

"And she hasn't made any noise about you and her previously bumping uglies?"

"Well, I only saw her today—"

"Dude, women don't sit on shit. If she was going to tell Morgan that you'd banged her, she would have by now."

"True."

And, if she had, I would've had a very pissed off Morgan in my office.

"She probably doesn't want Morgan to know as much as you don't. I mean, who would want their new boss knowing that they screwed the other CEO a week ago?"

"Yeah, you're right."

"I'm always right."

He lifts the ball, aims, and takes the shot. It goes in. "You've got nothing to worry about." He pats my shoulder as he passes me by, going to retrieve the ball.

"Yeah," I say, hoping to God he's right.

22

I decide to man up and have the meeting with Morgan. If I keep putting her off, she'll know something's up.

And Coop's right; I have nothing to worry about. I haven't done anything wrong. I slept with Sierra before she started working here. I couldn't have known she was going to apply for a job here and that Morgan was going to give it to her. I do need to have a conversation with Sierra to smooth things over, but I'll get to that later.

First, Morgan.

She's due in my office in ten minutes. It's close to lunchtime. I don't know if Morgan has lunch plans, but I had Chrissy go out and grab some pastries from the deli by the building. I know Morgan used to work at Starbucks, but I don't know if she's a coffee or tea drinker, so Chrissy makes up both and sets it up along with the pastries on the small meeting table I have in my office.

I'm replying to some outstanding emails when there's a tap on my door. It opens before I can say anything, revealing Morgan.

My eyes drink her up. I feel like I haven't seen her in forever—when, in reality, it was only yesterday morning.

She looks gorgeous.

Her hair is down and curled. She's wearing a fitted black scoop-neck top, which her tits look fantastic in, with a beige-and-black calf-length skirt that has a mid-thigh split over the left leg and a thick, chunky black belt that has a gold buckle.

I love the outfits with the leg split. They make my dick especially hard.

She has fucking great legs. Long, tan, and toned.

Morgan always wore pants in college, so I never got the privilege of seeing her legs. Probably a good thing, as it would have driven me nuts, knowing she had legs like that and I'd never get to touch them because she hated my guts.

And I'll still never get to touch them.

Sigh.

"Hi." She smiles, clutching an iPad to her chest.

Lucky iPad, being pressed up against those beauties.

"Hey. Take a seat." I gesture to the meeting table. "I just need to quickly finish this email."

"Sure. No problem."

I finish the email and press Send. Then, I get up from my desk, go over, and take a seat across from her.

"This is nice." She nods at the food.

"I didn't know if you had anything planned for lunch, so I had Chrissy bring something in just in case." I shrug to give off the air of casualness. Why though, I don't know. I shouldn't care if she had lunch plans or not.

Then, it suddenly occurs to me that I actually know nothing about Morgan's life outside of work.

I know she's not married or engaged because there's no ring, but that doesn't mean she doesn't have a boyfriend.

And women like her, smart and beautiful, don't stay single for long.

It shouldn't matter to me if she's dating someone or not. I only want to fuck her, and I'm not going to. So, it's a moot point.

"Just a sandwich at my desk, so this is great. Thanks."

She smiles, and something in my chest lights up.

What the hell is wrong with me?

I feel like a teenager on his first date. Not a grown-ass man in a business meeting with his co-CEO.

She pours herself a coffee. I like that she feels comfortable enough around me to do that.

"Coffee or tea for you?" she asks me.

"Coffee all the way. I don't drink tea. I just had Chrissy make it, as I wasn't sure what you liked."

"I'm like you, a coffee drinker. My body goes into shock if I go at least an hour without my fix."

"Noted."

I watch as she pours creamer into her cup.

"You take creamer?" she asks, holding it up.

"Please."

She pours creamer into my cup and then hands it over.

"Thanks. You get first dibs on the pastries, seeing as though you made coffee."

Looking over the plate with them, she bites her lip, and my dick twitches in my pants.

"Their éclairs are amazing," I tell her.

Her eyes meet mine. "And you wouldn't mind if I had it? There's only one."

I pick it up, put it on a napkin, and hand it over.

The smile she gives me is dazzling. It warms my insides.

She takes a bite. Her eyes close as she makes a sound of appreciation that has my dick instantly hard.

"That is so good," she murmurs, eyes opening as she chews.

I blink back at her. My mouth is suddenly dry. I grab my coffee and take a sip.

"Told you they were good," I finally get out.

"Don't tell me where Chrissy got them from; otherwise, I won't be able to stop myself from going and getting more."

I chuckle.

"Seriously, I'm going to have to do an extra ten minutes on the treadmill tomorrow to burn this off."

"You work out?" I pick up a raspberry macaron and take a bite.

I look at her, and she's staring back at me with a look in her eyes that I can't quite decipher. She nods and puts the éclair down on the napkin. Then, she gets another and wipes her hands on it.

"Do you use the office gym?"

"No." She curls her hand around her coffee cup and lifts it to her lips.

I watch her, confused. She was fine a second ago, but now, she's gone quiet. I don't know why. What I do know is that I don't like it.

"You should use the office gym. It's free to employees."

"I'll bear that in mind." Her eyes go down to the table, looking at the iPad she brought with her. She picks it up. "I don't want to take up too much of your time, so I'll get to the reason I'm here."

"Morgan," I say.

She lifts her eyes to me.

"Did I say something to upset you?"

"No. But we should get on with this, as I know you're busy, and I've another meeting with accounting to get to soon."

"Okay."

I pick up my coffee again and gesture for her to take the lead. She did call for this meeting after all.

Under
HER

"So, I have an idea about us branching out into the D-plus-sized area of the bra industry. And I know this is something you've probably thought of in the past, and I know the reasons you have never moved into the area, but just hear me out."

She's right. I did think of it and decided against it, mostly based on cost.

"I'm listening." I put my coffee down and give her my full focus.

"Okay, so there are lingerie companies that sell luxury bras for bigger-breasted woman, D-plus sizes. And companies like ours sell luxury bras for sizes A through D. But there are no companies that sell *all* sizes. The luxury-branded stores for D-plus-sized women are expensive, and I know the reason for this—cost of materials. That is why we and other lingerie companies have never moved into that area, but I think there's a way for us to do this without adding the big price tag to the D-plus sizes. No other luxury lingerie company has done this. We'd be the first and the only."

"So, you're saying that you have a cost-effective way for us to make D-plus-sized bras?"

"Yes."

"You've got my attention."

She smiles, and I feel like I've won something.

"So, a few years ago, Oscars sent me to Thailand to meet with some new potential suppliers. While I was there, I was wandering around a market in San Kamphaeng, and I came across a silk supplier."

"There are a lot of suppliers of silk in Thailand."

That's not me being an ass; it's the truth. Thailand is responsible for the global distribution of around seven hundred metric tons of silk per annum.

Even though Thailand is not the world's largest supplier of silk, they're still pretty significant.

And the fact that she thinks finding a silk supplier in Thailand is big news kind of worries me, as she comes from a clothing background.

"I'm well aware of that." She rolls her eyes. And I have to stifle a laugh. "And I also know of the cost the larger suppliers charge per meter. And I'm telling you that I know of a smaller supplier that will sell us silk charmeuse for fifty cents cheaper than what you're paying our current supplier from China."

That gets my attention. I sit up a little straighter and run the costs in my head.

"What's the name of the supplier?" I ask her.

"Ananda."

"I've never heard of them."

"Like I said, they're a small supplier. They sell more to local companies."

"Small would be a problem since we'd need large amounts of silk."

"But what if we stayed with our current supplier in China for the A-to-D-sized bras and bought the silk from Ananda for the D-plus sizes? In the beginning, that size would be in smaller demand until business increased."

"Does Oscars use them as a supplier?"

She shakes her head.

"Why not?"

"Because they weren't interested in a small supplier. They went with a bigger supplier with a quicker turnaround time even though the cost difference was significant. But I think we can work with the turnaround time. We're in no rush. We can place an order with Ananda and get the production moving. If the business grows for us, they can hire more staff to cope with the increasing demand, and because the product is cheaper, the cost for the D-plus bras will be the same as the A-to-D-sized bras. And, maybe going forward, if Ananda could expand their production size, then we could shift all purchases of silk charmeuse to them. But that's a conversation for another time. Right now, I really think we can do this, Wilder. I truly do."

Her enthusiasm is contagious. I feel it bleeding into me, giving me that thrill that can only come from a great business deal.

"What's the quality of the product like?" I ask her.

She puts her hand in the pocket of her skirt and pulls out a piece of red silk. She hands it to me. It has a flower stitched into it. "It's a handkerchief that Niran, the owner of Ananda, gave to me as a gift. It's a few years old, so the quality's not as good as it was. And don't worry; it's clean. I haven't wiped my nose on it today." She laughs softly.

I meet her eyes and laugh. "Good to know."

I run my fingers over the material, rubbing it between my fingers. "You said this is a few years old?"

"Yes," she replies.

"This is really good silk," I say to her.

"I know."

I look up at her, meeting her eyes. They're twinkling and smiling.

And, now, I'm getting hard again. At the thought of the new business and increase in sales but mostly because of *her*. Just her.

"I think you have something here," I tell her.

"Yeah?"

"Yeah." I nod. "I'm impressed. You've come up with a great business idea, and you've only been here just over a week."

"I'm awesome. What can I say?"

She gives a playful shrug, leaning back in her chair, and I chuckle.

"But, seriously, I was thinking of more cost-effective ways for bringing in materials when I was still at Oscars. I just brought that mindset here with me, and after looking at the supplier information over this past week, it just stood out to me, knowing about Ananda."

"It's brilliant."

"If it works."

"You losing confidence in your idea already?" I tip my head to the side, my lips lifting at the corners.

"No, just playing it safe until I have the deal in the bag. I don't want to get excited about it in case it doesn't happen."

"I get that." I nod, handing her the handkerchief back.

She tucks it into her pocket. "I'm guessing we need to present this idea to your mom and dad."

"Yeah, we should run it past them. They're technically still here in a chief officer capacity until the end of this week. And it is their company. I'll call them and set something up."

"Great." She picks up her iPad, pushes her chair back, and stands. "Well, just let me know when and where, and I'll be there."

I'm dismayed to see that she's leaving already. I feel like I need to keep her here even if just for a little longer.

Funny how I was dodging to see her, and now that I have her here, I don't want her to go.

"So, you're heading to another meeting now?" I stand, too, and walk over to my desk.

"Yep. Just with accounting."

"Tim or Justin?"

"Tim."

"You'll probably need another coffee then to keep you awake. The guy is boring as hell."

She giggles, and I fucking love the sound.

"Are you supposed to talk about your employees like that?"

"No. But the guy put me to sleep in a meeting once, so it's only fair to give you warning."

She laughs again. "Thanks for the heads-up. I'll make sure to have an industrial-strength coffee before I go in."

Under
HER

She's heading for the door. And I'm still not ready to let her go.

"So, any plans tonight?"

"Any plans tonight?"

Jesus. Could I be any more transparent?

She pauses and regards me with a tilt of her head. "Yep. I have a date with Jamie Fraser."

Disappointment lands in my chest like rocks.

"Jamie…is he your boyfriend?"

She barks out a laugh. "I wish." At my puzzled expression, she says, "He's a character in a show—*Outlander*. I'm guessing you've never heard of it."

"Nope. What's it about?"

"Kind of hard to explain, but it's about this woman who goes back in time to the 1700s in Scotland. And, once there, she meets Jamie Fraser. The hot Scottish warrior. It's based on a series of books."

"Sounds shite."

She laughs again.

"Does your boyfriend like it?"

That stops her laughter. And I want to punch myself in the face.

"Does your boyfriend like it?"

Fucking hell, Cross. Are you back in grade school?

She's appraising me with her eyes again. A small smile touches her lips. "I don't have a boyfriend." She gently shakes her head.

Pressure lifts off my chest.

"Oh. Cool. Well, have fun tonight with Jamie Fraser." I move around my desk and sit down.

She smiles, clutching the iPad to her chest. "I will. You, too. Have a good night, that is."

She turns, and I watch her leave, the door closing behind her.

Could I have been any more obvious just then? Jesus. I'm so off my game, it's ridiculous.

But I can't be on my game. Not with her. She's off-limits, no matter how much I don't want her to be.

M organ and I are having dinner with my mom and dad. When I called Mom to tell her that Morgan came up with a great idea for the business, she suggested a dinner meeting. I checked with Morgan to see if she was free, and she was, so we're meeting at my parents' favorite restaurant—Alinea.

I take a cab from my place. When I arrive, I'm the first one there. The hostess seats me, and I give the drink order—beer for me and a bottle of red for the table—to our waitress, who I'm ninety percent sure I've hooked up with before. When you sleep with as many women as I do, it's hard to keep track. But she looks familiar, and the way she keeps looking at me tells me that we've quite likely bumped uglies in the past.

"Hey." Morgan slips into the seat beside me, putting her clutch on the table.

I turn my eyes to look at her, and—

Holy fuck.

She's wearing a black lace dress. Her lips are red, hair down and poker straight, falling past her shoulders.

She looks fucking gorgeous.

It's going to be hard not to get hard tonight.

"Hey. You look nice." *Hot. Fuckable.*

"Oh. Thanks. You, too."

I'm wearing a dark red shirt, which is oddly the same color as her lips, and black pants.

"I was worried I was going to be the last one here. Traffic was a nightmare."

"You drove?"

"Took a cab." She smiles.

"What do you want to drink? I ordered a bottle of red for the table, but I wasn't sure what you'd want."

"I'm not a red-wine drinker. Gives me the worst hangovers."

I wave our waitress over. She approaches the table wearing a smile that dips when she sees Morgan sitting beside me, but Morgan doesn't seem to notice.

"What can I get you?" she asks Morgan.

"I'll have a vodka, soda, and lime, please."

Our waitress swivels on her heel and disappears off. But it's not her I'm looking at or thinking about. It's the woman sitting next to me.

The woman I work with.

The woman I want to fuck more than I've ever wanted to fuck anyone before.

"Did you mention anything about my idea to your parents?"

I shake my head. "I thought you'd want to tell them."

She smiles at me, her eyes warming, and I get the feeling again, like I've won something really important.

Our waitress appears with my beer, the red wine, and Morgan's drink.

"Thanks," Morgan says as the drink is put in front of her.

Her attention is back on me, but my eyes never left her.

We're staring at one another, and I feel like I should say something.

"Your lips match my shirt."

Really, Cross? That's the best you could come up with?

For fuck's sake.

She laughs softly. "So they do. At least, if I get lipstick on you, it won't show." Then, she realizes what she said. "Not that I plan on getting my lipstick on you. I just meant..." Her face is bright red now, and I'm as amused as I am turned on. "Oh Christ. You know what I meant." She picks up her drink and takes a big gulp.

I chuckle.

Actually, I don't know what she meant, but I'm not going to push her on it.

Even though I am enjoying seeing her squirm.

She puts her drink down but doesn't look at me.

I move a little closer, and in a lowered voice, I say, "If you did get lipstick on me, I wouldn't mind."

Her eyes whip to mine, but she doesn't look offended. She looks...interested, and there's a definite hint of desire in there, too. And, right now, it's hard to remember why I can't kiss the hell out of her.

Her breathing has gone shallow, like my own.

It feels like all the oxygen has been sucked out of this place along with everything else.

Nothing exists to me right now, except for her.

Her tongue darts out to wet her lips. My eyes are pulled to it.

I want to kiss her.

And I know she definitely wants me to.

I lift my eyes back to hers. "Before, when I said you looked nice, what I was actually thinking is that you looked gorgeous."

Her breath catches.

Fuck it. I'm going to do it. I'm going to kiss her.

"Darling!" The sound of my mother's voice pierces right through the moment.

Morgan's eyes widen with shock, and she moves away from me.

My heart is hammering in my chest.

"Mom, Dad," I say, rising to kiss my mom's cheek. I get a pat on the back in greeting from my dad.

Morgan stands, too. Her cheeks are flushed. "Hi, Mrs. Cross, Mr. Cross," Morgan greets them. I notice that her voice sounds as shaky as I feel.

"It's Frank and Nancy. How many times do I have to tell you?" my mom good-naturedly chides her. Then, she leans over and kisses Morgan's cheek.

My parents take the seats across from us. My dad pulls out my mom's chair for her and waits while she sits, like he always does.

"Sorry we're late," my mom says to us.

"You're not late," I tell her.

But I wish they had been. Then, I might have—no, I *would* have kissed Morgan. And I don't know whether to be pissed or relieved that I didn't get to kiss her. Because kissing Morgan would be a bad idea.

Not the kissing part. That would be amazing; I have no doubt about that. It's the *after* that would be bad. The awkwardness of the fact that we work together. We run the company together. I can't kiss her, and I definitely can't fuck her.

So, it's good that we were interrupted.

Our waitress appears again and asks for my parents' drink orders. My mom tells her that she's going to stick with the wine I already ordered. My dad orders a whiskey sour.

The whole time she's at the table, taking their orders, she's making sex eyes at me. But I'm more concerned with the fact that Morgan hasn't looked at me. Not once.

And it's pissing me off.

Under HER

I want to know what she's thinking.

Is she relieved that we didn't kiss? Or does she wish we had?

And I've turned into a thirteen-year-old girl.

Even still, I nudge her knee with mine, forcing her to look at me.

She lifts those gorgeous eyes to mine. They're expressionless. In complete contrast to how she was looking at me a few minutes ago.

I have an odd urge to see that desire in her eyes again.

"You okay?" I whisper to her.

She nods and then turns back to the table, opening one of the menus our waitress just brought.

Okay then. I'm guessing she's relieved we didn't kiss.

And if that doesn't just piss me right off.

"So, Morgan," my dad says, "Wilder tells us you've come up with a business idea."

"Frank, let's order our food before we talk business," my mom says.

I chuckle and pick up my own menu, trying to decide on what I want to eat, but it's hard to focus when I'm so distracted by Morgan sitting next to me. The scent of her perfume. The way she brushes her hair back with her hand as she leans forward to read the menu. Her finger running down the list of dishes. The way she nibbles her lip in thought.

I want to nibble that lip. No, I want to bite that lip.

I want to kiss that mouth and suck on her tongue and make her moan. And—

Stop.

I'm getting a hard-on, and I really don't want an erection while I'm sitting with my parents.

We all decide on food and place our orders with our waitress, who indecently drops a small piece of paper into my lap as she passes me by.

I look up at her, and she smiles and winks at me.

Yeah, not happening.

When I turn back, I see Morgan staring at me with barely concealed disgust in her eyes. She immediately looks away. I glance at my mom and dad to see if they saw, but they're too busy talking to realize that the waitress dropped me a note.

I want to tell Morgan that I have no intention of reading the note, which I'm guessing has her digits on it or a message like, *Meet me in the restroom in five minutes.*

This isn't the first time a waitress has dropped me a note.

But I can't say a damn thing to Morgan in front of my parents.

Even if I could say something, what would I say?
I'm not going to fuck the waitress because I want to fuck you.
Yeah, not likely.

But I don't want her to think that I will call the waitress after we're finished here. So, I pick the note up and tear it up into small pieces over the table.

"What's that you're tearing up?" my mom asks.

"Just a receipt," I tell her. Then, I drop the small pieces of paper into the glass candleholder that has a tea light candle burning in it, letting the pieces of paper burn up.

"Wilder!" my mom chastises. "You'll start a fire." She starts wafting her hands over the candle.

"That won't start a fire." My dad chuckles. "But you will, fanning it like that."

I chuckle as my mom pulls her hands back.

I look at Morgan. She doesn't look back at me, but I know she knows that I'm staring at her. And what she does do is smile.

And fuck if that smile doesn't make me feel good.

My dad picks up his drink and has a sip. "So, the food has been ordered. Now, I'm really interested in hearing this idea of yours, Morgan. It's the reason we're here."

Morgan smiles at my dad. "Okay."

She glances at me, and I give her a look of encouragement, which seems to brighten her eyes. She looks back to my parents and starts talking. She tells them everything she told me with the same level of enthusiasm that has me burning for her again.

I can't take my eyes off her as she talks. I'm enthralled.

I've never been this hot for a woman before. And I know I'm in trouble because I've realized that it's not only this woman's face and body that turns me on. It's her mind, too. She's smart as fuck. The way she lights up when she talks about work turns me on in a way no other woman ever has.

I might want to stick my tongue in her mouth and slide my cock up inside her pussy, but I want to talk to Morgan more. I want to *know* her.

She finishes talking, and my mom and dad are staring at her—smiles on their faces, exactly like I was wearing when Morgan first told me her idea.

"I knew you were smart, Morgan. That's why we wanted you to come work for us," my mom says. "But this…after being with us for only a short time." She looks at my dad, as if needing his help with words.

"We've talked about this in the past, wanting to break into this part of the market, but we could never make the figures work. But, if you're telling us that you have a way to make this work without losing product quality…" My dad leans back in his seat, drumming his fingers on the table. "Brilliant, Morgan. Really brilliant."

With Morgan bringing this great thing to the table, I was expecting to experience some level of jealousy on my part, purely because my mom and dad had brought her in and given her half of my job. And, now, she's living up to their high expectations, and so far, I've done fuck all, except for lust after her.

But I don't feel jealous. I actually feel…proud. Like Morgan's somehow mine to be proud of.

But she's not yours, assface. She's your business partner and nothing more.

Morgan looks at me, the praise lighting up her eyes.

And I've never wanted to kiss her more than I do right now.

I shove the thought away. "I told you they'd love it," I say to her.

Her smile softens on me.

My heart starts to thud in my chest.

Then, she looks away.

A moment later, our waitress turns up with our food, putting plates in front of us.

When the waitress is gone, my dad picks his knife and fork up. "I want you both on this." He points his knife at me and then Morgan.

I glance at Morgan to see how she feels about this. She's smiling, so I take that as a good thing.

"I want the both of you to draw up a proposal for this, pros and cons, and send them to me by Monday at the latest."

I meet Morgan's twinkling eyes.

"Sure thing," we both say at the same time.

I grin, and she smiles at me.

Dragging my eyes from her, I pick up my knife and fork.

And I won't deny that I'm thrilled at the prospect of having to work closely with Morgan on this over the next few days—maybe even the weekend, if I'm lucky.

What the hell? I'm actually wishing to miss out on my weekend fucks, so I can spend time working with Morgan.

Can the real Wilder Cross please stand up?

The only thing I can think is that my cock is in definite lust with her. That, or she's done some kind of voodoo to him.

That's the only explanation I have right now as to why I've turned into a Morgan-obsessed idiot.

13

We all leave the restaurant together. My parents have a car waiting. I'll hitch a ride with them. My condo is on Lake Shore, which is on the way to my parents' house on Gold Coast. They still live in the same house that I grew up in.

"Thanks for dinner," Morgan says to my mom and dad.

Mom kisses her on the cheek. "See you soon," Mom says to her, climbing in the car.

"I'm looking forward to seeing that proposal," my dad says to her. "You want a ride?" Dad asks me, climbing in next to my mom.

"Yeah, I'll just grab Morgan a cab."

"Oh, no need. I'm going to walk. I only live on Lincoln." She thumbs over her shoulder.

"I thought you got a cab here?" I say stupidly.

She smiles. "I came from the office. I was working late."

"Okay. Well, I'll walk you home."

"You don't need to. It's not far."

"I don't give a shit if it's five steps away. I'm walking you," I firmly tell her. "I'm walking Morgan home," I tell my parents, leaning into the car. "I'll talk to you later."

I shut the car door.

I turn to Morgan as my parents' car pulls away into traffic.

"You really don't have to walk me home," she says to me.

"I'm not letting you walk the streets of Chicago alone at night."

"It's not that late."

"Mmhmm. Okay. So, you think murderers don't start work until it's super late?"

"I actually didn't know that murdering was a profession." She gives me a dry look.

"You're hilarious. And I'm serious, Morgan. You shouldn't be walking around the city on your own at night."

When I look at her, a smile is tugging at her lips, and she's shaking her head at me.

"What?"

"I just didn't realize that you had such strong feelings about women walking Chicago's streets alone."

"I don't. I just care about you walking these streets alone."

Something flashes across her face. It's not happiness at my words. If anything, she looks annoyed, but it's gone too quickly for me to know for sure.

She stares ahead, wrapping her arms over her chest.

She isn't wearing a coat, and a slight chill is in the air.

I don't ask if she's cold because something tells me that, right now, she'd reject the offer of my jacket.

So, instead, I slide my jacket off, keeping pace with her, and I step closer and hang it over her shoulders.

She stops abruptly. Her eyes flash to mine.

"You looked cold," I say gently.

Her lips press together, like she's about to argue with me, so I'm surprised when she says, "Thank you." Her words are soft, and they curl in around my chest and settle there.

She slips her arms into my jacket.

It's huge on her. And the sight of her wearing my jacket sets off something primal inside me.

I want to pick her up, carry her off to my lair, and do dirty, dirty things to her all night long.

Heat flares in my groin, and I have to bite back a moan at the images flashing through my head.

Morgan starts walking again, and I follow, falling in step beside her.

I shove my hands in my pants pockets to stop myself from doing something stupid, like grabbing her and kissing her right here on the street.

We walk in silence for a while. I can't think of a thing to say that doesn't consist of the words *kiss* and *fuck*, so I keep my mouth shut, as I know I can't do either of those things with her, no matter how much I want to.

My parents love her, and I know they would kick my ass to hell and back if I screwed things up with her working for the business.

And I know me. I'd screw things up.

Business, I'm great at. Women, not so much. Well, I'm great at fucking them, but anything beyond that? Nope.

"Your mom and dad seemed...happy with my idea," she says softly.

I slide my eyes to her. "They are happy with your idea. *More* than happy."

The smile that appears at my words sparks alive every sexual feeling in my body like nothing ever has before.

If her smile can do that to me, then I can only imagine what it would feel like to be inside her.

Why does the one woman who excites me this much have to be the one woman I can't touch?

I try to tell myself that that's the reason. Because I can't touch her.

But it's not.

It's *her*.

I can feel my cock start to swell in my pants. In an attempt to direct my thoughts elsewhere, I say, "So, I know you lived in Evanston when we were at Northwestern and you live in Chicago now, but where are you from originally?"

"Decatur," she says.

"Can't say I've ever been."

"You're not missing much." Her lips lift at the corners.

"You didn't like it?"

"No, I love it. It's home. But it's not as"—she wafts her hands around, as though trying to find the words—"exciting as Chicago, if that's the right word to use."

"Exciting is as good as any word." *You're exciting. You excite the hell out of me.*

"You're from Chicago, right?" she says. It doesn't sound so much like a question but more like a statement.

"Yep. Born and bred."

We continue walking on in silence, but it's not uncomfortable. It's actually nice.

I can't remember the last time I walked a woman home like this—without the promise of anything at the end of it.

There probably hasn't ever been a time. Because, when there's me and a woman in the mix, there's always sex at the end of it.

Except with her.

It's different. And I like it.

I like her.

"So…this is me." She comes to a stop outside a three-story brownstone on Lincoln.

Looking up at the building, I ask, "Which apartment is yours?"

"Top floor."

"I'll see you upstairs."

"I'll be fine." She laughs softly. "My downstairs neighbor, Mrs. Bigly, is like a rottweiler. No one gets in this building if they don't live here."

"So, she wouldn't let me in?"

"Definitely not." She grins up at me.

"I'm sure I could charm my way in."

I wink at her, and she laughs.

"I'd like to see you try. Mrs. Bigly's immune to bullshit."

That makes me laugh. Her eyes are sparkling with amusement. Warmth spreads across my chest.

Fuck, I want her.

"Oh, your jacket." She slips it off and hands it to me.

I want to tell her to keep it, but there's no reason for me to say that without it seeming odd, so I take it from her.

"So…" She takes a step back, and I want to follow her. "Thanks for walking me home."

"Anytime."

She seems to hesitate. Then, she turns and walks up the steps. I watch her go. When she reaches the top, she gets her key from her clutch and unlocks the door. She opens it and then pauses before turning back to me.

"I had a good time tonight."

I smile at her. "Me, too."

"Good night, Wilder."

"Night, Morgan."

I watch her go inside, and the door shuts safely behind her before I leave.

I see a taxi light heading my way, so I step out and flag it down.

The taxi stops, and I get in.

"Lake Shore," I tell the driver.

The driver has the air conditioner on full blast, so I pull my jacket on. It smells of her, and my dick is instantly flying at full mast.

For fuck's sake.

I want her so badly. And it's getting harder not to act on my feelings. Leaving her just then was tough. I wanted nothing more than to kiss her. Take her inside her apartment and fuck her senseless.

But I can't. No matter how much I want inside that gorgeous body of hers, I have to stay away.

And I hate that.

Maybe I should stick with my original plan of getting her ousted from the company. Then, I'd get my job back, and I'd also get to sleep with her.

Yeah, and that's probably the most selfish and dickish thought you've ever had, Cross.

As much as I hate to admit it, she's already shown herself to be a valuable asset to the company.

God, why didn't I just fuck her all those years ago in college?

Because she hated you, dickface.

If I could go back in time, I'd tell eighteen-year-old Wilder to change eighteen-year-old Morgan's mind about him, making her see that he wasn't the total prick she thought he was, and then I'd tell him to fuck her for a week straight because a day would definitely not be enough.

But, unfortunately, I don't have a fucking time machine, so I'm stuck in my perpetual hell of wanting her and not being able to have her.

I really need to get laid.

But I know, even if I went out to a bar now, picked up some chick, and screwed her for hours on end, it wouldn't change anything. I'd still feel the same frustration.

Because my cock wants Morgan.

I want Morgan.

14

I step out of the shower in my office bathroom. I grab a towel, rub it over my hair to dry it off, and then wrap it around my waist.

I did a workout in the office gym, and I was sweaty as fuck afterward. There are showers down there, but I prefer to use my own. And it meant that I could jerk off.

That has become a regular occurrence for me over this past week.

Working with Morgan on the proposal for her D-plus bras meant I was with her a lot. And, when the proposal was done, we put it forward to my parents. Of course, they gave the go-ahead, so we're well underway on project D-plus bras, meaning I'm going to be working with Morgan even more.

And, as awesome as that is and as much as I love being with her and working with her, getting to know her better, the need to fuck her is becoming unbearable. And the only way to keep it under control and stop myself from hitting on her is to jerk off regularly.

I tried getting it on with someone else when I went out with the boys on Saturday night—this chick called Mandy or Brandy or something to that effect. She was a dancer and was all kinds of flexible, as she was keen to demonstrate. But I just wasn't into it. So, after getting her off because I felt like it was the least I could do, I left without even banging her.

The whole time, I'd felt like I was trying to talk myself into eating store-brand candy because it was all that was on offer when what I really wanted was Hershey's.

Morgan is my Hershey's.

And, apparently, I'm on a motherfucking diet.

I stand in front of the bathroom mirror. It's steamed up. I wipe a hand over it, clearing it, and stare at myself.

I can see the lines of stress caused by my sexual frustration etched around my eyes.

Ugh.

Solely wanting Morgan is even causing me premature aging.

For fuck's sake.

I drop my forehead against the mirror and let out a groan.

I'm so fucking horny, it hurts.

I stand back, away from the mirror, and decide to get dressed.

But, when I open the door and step out of my bathroom and into my office, as I left my work clothes in there, I'm halted in my tracks, finding Sierra sitting on the edge of my desk, waiting for me.

"Hi," I say slowly, cautiously.

"Hi." She smiles, like it's not odd that she's here, in my office.

"Where's Chrissy?" I ask, my eyes going to the door, as if I can magic her up just by looking at it.

She shrugs. "Lunch, if I had to guess."

Great. So, I'm here alone with her. And I'm dressed in nothing but a towel.

I haven't had a chance to have a talk with Sierra. I've been too busy. Mostly working with Morgan on the proposal. And, on the few occasions that I have seen Sierra, I've been with Morgan, and that's definitely not a chat I'm having around her.

"So, um…what are you doing in here, Sierra?" I curl my fingers into the waistband of my towel, getting a firm hold on it.

"I want to talk."

And, from the way her eyes drag down my body, pausing on my cock area, and how she grazes her teeth over her lower lip, I know talking's not the only thing she wants to do.

As if my life isn't fucked up enough as it is, I now have to deal with this.

"Well, just let me get dressed, and we can talk."

I start to move across the room to grab my clothes, but she hops off my desk, blocking my path.

"Sierra…" My tone is a warning.

But it's one that she doesn't heed because she advances on me. I back up because I don't know what the fuck else to do, and before I know it, my back is against the wall, and she's pressed up against me.

"I thought you'd come for me, but you haven't, and I'm bored of waiting, Wild. So, I'm here to take what I want. And I want you."

Ah, shit.

She trails a finger down my chest, and I catch hold of her wrist.

She doesn't look pissed off. She looks…excited. I guess she likes it rough. Not that I remember anything from that night.

"It's not going to happen, Sierra."

Her eyes flicker with dislike, but she doesn't move away.

"I'm your boss."

"Morgan's my boss," she counters.

I have to hold back a sigh.

"I'm CEO; therefore, I'm your superior. And I don't fraternize with the staff. Ever."

"You've already fraternized with me."

She grins and bites the corner of her lip. I don't find it remotely sexy. She's no Morgan.

"You didn't work here then," I tell her.

She moves even closer to me, and now, there isn't any space left between her body and mine.

"No one has to know," she whispers, inching up onto her toes. "We could fuck right now. You could go *Wild* on me, and no one would ever know."

I bite back another sigh. I'm trying to be as diplomatic as possible, but this chick just isn't getting it.

"I'd know. And it just doesn't sit right with me. Sure, we had fun once. But I don't want to go there again with you."

"Your cock says different." She reaches down and squeezes my erect cock through the towel.

Of course I'm hard. I haven't had sex in a while, and a good-looking woman is pressed up against me. As a man, it's almost impossible to have a hot woman press herself up against you and you not go hard. My equipment might be faulty at the moment, but it hasn't stopped working. The rocket fuel is still burning; it's just failing to take off after countdown.

Well, unless you go by the name of Morgan Stickford, and then my cock will take off at warp speed. It'd fly to the fucking moon and back to get in her pussy.

I grab hold of Sierra's other wrist and pull her hand off my cock.

So, now, I have both her arms in my hands. And she's clearly not fucking getting it because she smiles in a way that I'm sure she thinks is sexy, but it's doing nothing for me. Then, she presses her hips firmly against my cock and grinds against me.

And wouldn't you just fucking know it?

My towel drops to the floor.

And it's at that exact fucking moment when there's a tap on my door, followed by the sound of Morgan's voice as she opens it up and walks in. "Hey, sorry to—" Her words instantly cut off at the sight of me and Sierra.

I'm up against the wall, naked as the day I was born, with Sierra pressed up against me, my hands wrapped around her wrists, holding her.

For fucking fuck's sake.

In the long seconds that pass, a multitude of emotions flash through Morgan's eyes. Anger, disgust, disappointment...but the one emotion I get stuck on is hurt.

She's hurt by the sight of me with Sierra.

Is that because she wants me like I want her?

Everything is telling me yes.

And I don't know whether to feel elated or fucking terrified by that thought.

"Morg—" I don't even get a chance to finish saying her name.

She turns and walks out of my office, slamming the door behind her.

"Oops." Sierra giggles.

My eyes narrow, lit with anger. I firmly move her back and bend down to get my towel off the floor, wrapping it back around my waist.

I stare her down. "Get the fuck out of my office. Now. And, if I ever catch you in here like that again, you're fired."

"You can't just fire me." Her hands go to her hips, eyes wide.

"I can. And I will." I take a menacing step toward her. "If you ever cross the line like that again, I'll have your ass out on the street before you can say *pink slip*." I walk over and pick up my shirt from where I left it on the sofa along with the rest of my clothes. "Oh, and sexual harassment charges aren't just against men, you know."

Worry sparks in her eyes. "You wouldn't…"

"I would. And good luck explaining to Morgan what just happened."

Defiance narrows her eyes along with something else, something I'm not quite sure of…until she says, "Well, I guess I'll just have to tell Morgan the truth—that we've fucked already. I'm sure she'd love to hear all about that. And maybe I'll tell her that we've been screwing all along." She smirks, trailing her finger over her cleavage.

The bitch. She knows I have a thing for Morgan. *Shit.*

I shrug like I don't give a fuck. But the truth is, my heart is hammering in my chest.

I yank my shirt on and do up the buttons. "Go home," I tell her, my voice hard. "I'll talk to Morgan."

She smiles like she's won something. Because she has. She's won this round.

"I'll see you in the morning, Wild." Then, she sashays out of my office, the door closing firmly behind her.

Morgan
Twelve and a Half Years Ago

You can try to ignore something...someone...your own feelings. But you're not really ignoring them; you're just pretending you are.

And I've gotten really good at pretending.

Pretending that I can't stand Wilder Cross. Pretending that my heart doesn't beat a little faster every time I see him. Pretending that my heart doesn't sink when I see him with a girl.

Pretending that my crush hasn't turned into real feelings for him. Because how can I have feelings for a jackass like him? It doesn't make sense. So, therefore, the feelings can't be real. Right?

See, I'm damn good at pretending. And I figure, if I keep on like this, one day, my pretense will just stick. It'll become reality.

Avoidance is a great tool. If I don't see him much, then I don't have to fake it at all.

So, wouldn't you just know that Wilder and I have been paired together to do an assignment for our Economics class?

We only need to do one study session together, so we can figure out which part each of us will do. But the thought of one session—just me and him, one-on-one—feels like the best and worst kind of torture.

I'm great at pretending to myself and everyone else, but I don't know if I'll be able to pretend if it's just Wilder and me. And he can't ever know that I have feelings for him.

God, could you imagine the fun he and his buddies would have with that?

Stick-Up-Her-Ass-Ford has a thing for Wilder Cross.

Yeah, that's the nickname that Wilder has for me. Not the most original. He doesn't say it to my face, but I have ears. And I can't say that it doesn't bother me because it does.

Not that Wilder cares about my feelings.

The only thing he cares about is sleeping with as many girls as possible.

He screws just about anything with a vagina. And, of course, they're all slim, gorgeous girls because Wilder Cross doesn't do anything over a size four.

At the remembrance of what he said that night, I breathe through the ache in my chest that I still get, even now.

So, I guess you could say that I'm not looking forward to this study session with him.

Under HER

And, when my boss asked me if I could stay a few more hours, as one of the girls had called in sick, I said yes. Not only would the extra cash come in handy, but it also delayed the inevitable a little longer.

And, now, straight from work, I'm on my way to Wilder's frat house, which is where we're meeting. I did try to book a room at the library, but they were all full, and I definitely didn't want Wilder in my dorm room. The dorm room that I no longer share with Tori.

She left a month ago. She got knocked up. Not by Wilder. By one of the guys on the football team. She went back home, wherever that is.

So, I have the room to myself. But the last time Wilder was in my room, it didn't end so well for me, so, yeah, not happening.

The only option left was his frat house. We can work in the kitchen or whatever.

As I walk toward the address he gave me, I hear thumping music coming from inside. As I get closer, I see people out front, on the porch, drinks in their hands.

He's having a party?

He knew I was coming. Granted, I'm two hours later than I originally said I would be, but I emailed him to let him know I had to change the time. And it's only eight thirty now, and this party looks like it's been going on for a while.

I hesitate, not sure what to do. Do I go in and find him? For what reason? We can't exactly work while there's a party happening.

But, now, I'm pissed. Because, if he was having a party, then he should've let me know, and we could've rearranged. But he definitely didn't let me know because I quickly checked my email at work before I left, and there was nothing from him. I haven't received a text or phone call from him either.

God, does he not ever take anything seriously?

My annoyance quickly turns to anger.

And that's what has me marching up the front lawn and up the steps to the porch and through the open front door.

The house is full of people, drinking, dancing, and making out. Girls are wearing skimpy dresses, and I'm standing here in my work uniform.

I feel a stab of envy. I don't party often...well, ever. I'm too busy with school and work to have a social life. And I'm not exactly rolling with the popular crowd, so my party invites are pretty rare...well, nonexistent.

I glance around, looking for Wilder. I see a few people I know from classes but no Wilder.

I walk through the living room and to the kitchen. Still no sign of him.

By this point, I'm pissed off and ready to go home, but I want to find him, so I can yell at him.

I grab a random guy and ask if he knows where Wilder is.

"Out back," he tells me.

I make my way through the kitchen and let myself out back. There are some people out here, but I can't see Wilder.

Then, I hear a female giggle to my left. I turn my head to find a pretty brunette pressed up against the house with Wilder leaning into her.

A flash of jealousy lances across my chest.

Almost as if he hears my pain, his head turns, and his eyes focus on me.

A smile creeps onto his lips. But it's not a nice smile.

"A little late, aren't you?"

"Late?" My brows furrow.

He steps away from the girl and turns to me. "Yeah, about two hours too late for our study session."

"I emailed you to let you know I couldn't make it and that I'd be coming now."

His head tips to the side. "I didn't get an email, Stickford. And, FYI, people generally text each other now. You know, cell phones." He pulls his phone from his pocket and waves it at me.

The brunette giggles, which just pisses me off even more.

"I know, asshole. But I didn't have access to my phone at the time, so I emailed."

My phone is in my bag, but I'm not going to tell him that I couldn't text or call him because I'm out of credits on my prepay phone, and I don't have any spare cash to put some credits on it until I get paid in a few days.

It was minutes for my phone or food. Crazy gal that I am, I opted for food.

Wilder takes a step closer to me and away from the brunette he was just pressed up against. "So, what was so important that you had to miss our meeting then? Wait, let me guess." He clicks his fingers and then points at me. "I know. You were with Professor Weller, getting your nose surgically removed from her ass because it'd been stuck up there so long that hemorrhoids started to grow out your nostrils."

The girl bursts out laughing. And I can feel my face heating with embarrassment.

"Surely, you couldn't have been doing something fun, like getting laid, because you don't know how to have fun, Stickford."

"You're an ass. And I'm done here."

I push past him, ignoring the laughing brunette, and I all but run down the steps off the back porch. I'm speed walking down the side of the house when a hand catches my arm.

I whirl around to see Wilder.

His eyes are lit in a way I've never seen before. It makes both my legs tremble and my heart beat faster.

"You could have called to let me know you'd be late, Morgan."

He rarely calls me Morgan. It throws me off balance for a moment.

I pull my arm from his hand, needing him to stop touching me because I can feel my mask starting to fade.

I hate that he has this effect on me.

How can I want such a mean, jumped-up asshole, whose sole aim in life is to screw as many girls as possible? It makes no sense to me. *He* makes no sense to me.

"I couldn't call you," I tell him through thin lips. "I was at work. My boss offered me extra hours, as one of the other girls had called in sick, and I couldn't *not* take them because I need the money. We're not all born with a rich mommy and daddy who can pay our bills for us."

His eyes narrow on me, but he doesn't say anything for a long moment.

Then, he just turns and starts to head back to the party.

"We need to rearrange our study session," I call to his back. "I'm not failing this class because of you."

He stops and turns back to me. His eyes look dark. "I did the work. Well, my half of it. Because you didn't turn up, I made the decision of who should do what. I'll email my part to you tomorrow, so there's no need for us to meet again."

I should be relieved. But I'm not.

"What if I don't want to do the part that you're giving me?"

He laughs, but it's a hollow sound. "Then, complain to Professor Weller. I know you have no problem doing that because she pulled me aside the other day to ask me what the issue was between you and me. Said that you'd been to see her and asked to be reassigned to a different partner. And you know what I told her?" He takes long strides back toward me until he's so close that I have to tip my head back to look into his face, which looks clouded with anger.

Under
HER

"I told her that I don't have a fucking clue what I ever did to make you dislike me." His voice is a harsh sound in my ear.

I swallow roughly, and he takes a step back and runs his hand through his hair.

"But you know what else I told her?"

Dumbly, I shake my head.

"I told her that I don't care. Whatever your problem with me is, well, it's your problem and not mine." And then he's gone, striding off back to the party. Back to his brunette.

"But that's the problem," I whisper to his back. "You didn't care. You hurt my feelings, and you just didn't care."

16

I don't bother to knock on Morgan's office door. I just walk straight in.

Her head comes up from her computer, her eyes narrowing with anger on me.

I have flashbacks to college and her looking at me that exact same way on many occasions.

Dislike and disdain.

And, just like it bothered me then—not that I ever let her know that—it bothers me now. Even more so.

"I'm busy," she says.

"This won't take a minute. What you just saw in my office wasn't what you thought it was."

She barks out a laugh. "So, you weren't just about to fuck my assistant."

"No." I grit my teeth. "I'd just come out of my bathroom after showering and—"

"Often take showers during the day, do you?"

"When I've just done a workout in the gym on my lunch hour, yes, I do." I pause, gritting my teeth. I take a deep breath in through my nose and then exhale it out. "Look, Sierra and I have…a past. A short past. We slept together once before she started working here."

"And you just didn't bother to tell me?"

"I didn't think it was any of your business."

She laughs. "Typical, Wilder."

"What the hell is that supposed to mean?"

"It means, you never think further than the end of your cock."

I grind my teeth. "Honestly, I didn't want to cause a problem, and I knew, if I told you that I'd slept with her the night before you came in for that first meeting—"

"Hang on." She holds up a hand. "Sierra was the reason you were late for our meeting? She's the one who left that note on your shirt?"

I realize what I just let slip, and my balls shrivel up into my body. "Yes."

She lets out a sound of disbelief, shaking her head.

"I would never have touched her if I had known she was going to start working here."

"Yet you were just naked in your office with her pressed up against you."

"That was all her. She was waiting for me. I hadn't invited her, and I sure as hell didn't want her there. But she wasn't taking no for an answer."

"So, she overpowered you and pressed you up against the wall?"

"I wouldn't say overpowered—"

She laughs derisively, cutting me off. "You can go now. I have work to do."

"Don't fucking do that. Don't dismiss me like I'm your assistant."

"Well, don't screw my actual assistant in your office in the middle of the day, and maybe I won't!" she yells, rising to her feet, hands pressed to the desk, her face red, eyes bright with anger.

"I didn't screw her!"

"Only because I interrupted you!"

"I wasn't going to do a goddamn thing with her! Aside from the fact that she works here and I never touch employees, I never ride the same roller coaster twice."

"God, you're disgusting. Same game, different place. You're working your way through the female population of Chicago just like you worked your way through Northwestern."

"Except for you, Morgan. I never worked my way through you."

Her jaw clenches, working angrily. "Only because I saw right through you. God." She laughs. "Same old Wilder Cross. And here I was, thinking you'd changed. You sure had me fooled."

"What the hell is that supposed to mean?"

"It means, you're still the same shallow, self-centered, womanizing asshole that you were in college!"

"Yeah, and you're the same stuck-up, judgmental bitch that you always were!"

"Fuck you," she spits.

"Original." I laugh. "But maybe that's the problem, Morgan. Maybe you want to fuck me, and you can't. Maybe that's been the problem all along. You wanted to screw me in college, too, and that was why you were so bent out of shape all the time."

Her eyes narrow like lasers. I know I'm being a dick, overstepping the mark, but she pushes my buttons like no one. She's always been able to push my buttons.

"God, I hate you," she bites.

I narrow my gaze on her. "The feeling is one hundred percent mutual, sweetheart."

"Don't call me that. I'm not your sweetheart."

"Thank God because, if you were, my balls would have frozen off by now."

Her eyes close, and I hate that I can't see what she's thinking. She exhales slowly through her nose and then opens her eyes.

"Anything else?" Her tone is so even, you wouldn't think we were just tearing each other to shreds.

"No."

"Good."

Her eyes move to her office door, and I take the blatant hint.

I've just opened the door when her voice hits my back. "Where's Sierra?"

I glance at her over my shoulder. "I sent her home for the rest of the day."

She laughs softly. "Figures."

"What does that mean?"

"It means that you do what's best for you and screw everyone else."

That's like a match to my simmering flame. "Fuck you, Morgan. You don't know the first thing about me. You don't get to come in here and speak to me like this after five minutes of working here. Yeah, you might be co-CEO or what-the-hell-ever, but this company is mine, and irrespective of what you think just happened with Sierra in my office, I deserve some fucking respect from you."

She sniffs. "Respect is earned."

I give her a pointed look. "Yeah, it fucking is." Then, I spin on my heel and slam her office door behind me.

I march to my office, ignoring Chrissy, who's finally reappeared at her desk.

I slam my office door shut, stride over to my desk, and sit down in my chair.

I'm seething.

Under HER

Who the hell does she think she is? She might be hot, but she's still a bitch. God, I hate her.

Well, I don't hate her. But I want to.

I'm sick of lusting over her.

And, after today, with her talking to me like that, screw that, I'm done.

I want her gone. From this office and out of my life and my thoughts.

My initial instinct to get rid of her was the right one.

And I will do whatever is necessary to make that happen.

I need ideas on how to get rid of her from here, but I can't think of any because my mind is too damn twisted up with her to think straight.

I turn to my computer and open up my email. I start a new email, addressed to Coop and Dom. My fingers angrily hit the keys as I type out a message to them

> **Me: SOS. I need ideas on how to get rid of her.**

Coop replies almost immediately.

> **Coop: Am I right in guessing that *her* is Morgan?**

Me: Yep.

> **Coop: I thought you were getting on okay with her?**

Me: I was, but then she caught me in my office with Sierra.

> **Coop: Were you fucking her?**

Me: No, asshole, I wasn't. And I wasn't planning on fucking her either. Sierra turned up in my office when I got out of the shower, and she tried to seduce me.

> Coop: You should have fucked her.

Me: Dude. Can you stay focused here?

> Coop: Okay. Sorry...but what do I need to focus on?

Me: Getting rid of Morgan.

> Dom: Just playing catch-up. And, dude, you want to get rid of Morgan? You don't mean...kill her, right? Because I love you, man, like a brother, but I'm too pretty for jail.

> Coop: No, I'm too pretty for jail. You'd just be the nerd they beat up every day for fun.

> Dom: Fuck you.

> Coop: You're not my type, nerd boy.

Under HER

Me: Jesus Christ! Can we please get back on topic?

But, before I do...no, Dom, I don't mean I want to kill Morgan. You really need to stop watching *Cold Case*. It's scrambling your brain.

I want her gone from the business, as in fired. But I don't know how to make that happen. Especially not now, as she came up with this really great idea for the business, and my mom and dad love her even more for it.

> **Coop: So, sabotage her great idea. Make her look incompetent. Then, your mom and dad will fire her.**

That makes me sit back. *Could I actually do that? Sabotage her business idea?*

No. Not only for the fact that I would never do anything to hurt the company, but I also couldn't do that to her.

Me: No...I can't do that.

I shut my email down and turn my chair so that I can look out at the city below me.

I feel a lot calmer than I did before, but I haven't changed my mind.

I still want Morgan gone from here. I want my life to go back to how it was before she came here and messed everything up.

I just need to figure out how to make that happen. I need a plan of action of how to get Morgan fired that doesn't involve fucking up the Ananda deal.

Morgan is about to learn that there's only one boss at Under Her Lingerie.

And that's me.

It's official. I've reverted back to my childhood ways.

When I was in kindergarten, I had this crush on Sandy Harman. She was the prettiest girl in my class. And, of course, like any other five-year-old who had a crush on a girl, I was mean to her. Pulled her pigtails, stole her juice box at lunch—that kind of thing.

Well, I'm reduced back to the days of Sandy Harman, except it's with Morgan now.

She might be hotter than the sun, but she's also the devil.

The next day after our argument, I was willing to be civil—until I get rid of her, that is. But Morgan apparently wasn't on the same lines as me.

We had a morning meeting with finance. And then she accidentally stood on my foot on the way out of the conference room.

And she just happened to be wearing a pair of five-inch Louboutin heels.

Forget the fact that those are some serious come-fuck-me shoes, and in any other circumstances, I'd be lusting over her in those shoes.

But, if you've never had a five-inch stiletto heel drive its way into your foot, well, let me just tell you how much it hurts. A fuck of a lot.

A week later, I still have the bruise on my foot to prove it.

Let's just say, I was pissed off after that little incident. So, I might have replaced that powdered milk shit that she puts in her coffee with confectioners sugar.

The sound of her choking and spluttering in the kitchen was the highlight of my day.

Well, until I came into work the next day and found that someone had changed the password on my computer, locking me out of my own damn PC. It didn't take long for IT to sort it out, but it was more the inconvenience that pissed me off.

I only wish I were there to hear all the calls she must be receiving about the ad for the used vibrator, free to a good home, that had been listed on Craigslist yesterday with her name and number.

I know I'm an ass, but she deserves it.

I'll take the ad down after this morning's staff meeting. I reckon a day of annoying phone calls is enough payback for locking me out of my computer.

Maybe, if I'd put as much effort into coming up with a plan to get her out of here as I did with playing stupid pranks on her, then she might have been on her way out the door by now.

Morgan's cell lights up with a call on the table in front of her. That's the third time her phone has gone off since the meeting started forty minutes ago.

She sighs and reaches over, canceling the call.

I stifle a laugh.

Fuck, I love Craigslist.

Under HER

I focus back on my mom's voice. She's saying something about this year's targets.

I was originally leading this morning's meeting, but somehow, my mom ended up taking over, so I took the only available seat, which was next to Morgan.

My parents officially retired last week. But they've both been in the office every day for one reason or another. I know it has nothing to do with thinking that Morgan and I aren't capable of running the company—even if, at the moment, that's questionable, as we can barely hold a conversation without throwing barbs at each other. But I know it's because my parents are finding it hard to let go.

Her phone goes off again, and I can't help but lean close to her and whisper in her ear, "You should probably get that. You don't want to miss out on a potential sale."

She makes a cute growly sound under her breath. Then, do you know what she does? She fucking nips me. Hard. Right on that tender part of my arm, near my armpit.

I bark out a curse, and everyone in the room turns to look at me.

"Everything okay, Wilder?" my mom asks me, brows furrowed.

"Yep." I clear my throat. "Everything's fine. Carry on."

My mom looks at me for a long moment. Then, she resumes talking, and all eyes focus back on her.

"That wasn't very nice," I whisper under my breath.

"You deserved it, asshole."

"Bitch."

"Why don't you go fuck yourself, Cross?"

I laugh softly. "Like you do with your vibrator? No, thanks."

"I don't even—" Her voice pitches, and she pauses, reining it back in when Bob from HR looks across the table at her.

"Go to hell," she whispers to me when Bob looks away.

I chuckle quietly. "That's rich, coming from the devil herself."

I see her hands curl into fists on the table, making me laugh again. And I realize just how turned on I am right now.

I'm getting off on making her mad.

Jesus, I can't win here. Will I ever stop lusting after her?

Yes. When I get her out of here.

As soon as this meeting's done, I'm going to work out a plan of action—after I take down the Craigslist ad, that is.

"Okay. So, that's it for today. Unless anyone has anything to add?" my mom says, finishing up the meeting. "No? Well, everyone have a good rest of the day."

I pick my cell up from the table and put it in my pocket.

"Wilder, Morgan, have you got a minute?" my mom says from the front of the room.

I pause. So does Morgan.

Shit. Does my mom know about all the stupid shit Morgan and I have been pulling on each other?

"Sure," I say at the same time Morgan says, "Of course."

We wait for the room to clear, and then my mom closes the door.

"What's up?" I ask, sitting on the edge of the table.

Morgan is standing at the opposite side of the table from me.

"Well, I was talking with your dad—Frank," she adds, looking at Morgan, "last night about the Ananda deal, and even though everything seems to be running on schedule, we just want you to go out to the factory and check to make sure everything is running as they say it is."

"You want me to go to Thailand to do a production check?" I ask.

I've never been to Thailand before. Could be fun.

I can fuck some hot Europeans and probably even some Australian backpackers while I'm there, tending to business.

Two birds, one stone.

My sex life has been on a downward spiral as of late. As in it's not happening—at all. My cock has gone on some kind of hiatus, thanks to Morgan.

So, this trip to Thailand, away from the office and Morgan, will be just what I need to get my cock back on his game.

I'm actually smiling, thinking of all the hot sex I can have in Thailand, when my mom says, "Yes. But not just you, Wilder. I want Morgan to go with you. I want the both of you to go out to Thailand and do the production check together."

And, just like that, my happy thoughts are obliterated.

A nd that's how I find myself, four days later, in a taxi with Morgan, on our way to our hotel in San Kamphaeng after the longest flight of my life. And, when I say *longest*, I mean, because of Morgan. Sure, we had to fly from Chicago to Bangkok and then take a flight to Chiang Mai.

But I've done long flights before.

It was made unbearably longer by the fact that Morgan wouldn't speak to me unless it was work-related. According to her, we don't need to talk about work until tomorrow, so there's no need for us to talk at all. And, when I have tried to coax her into speaking to me, all I've gotten back is, *Fuck off, I hate you*, or *Can't you just hurry up and die already?*

So, clearly, I'm in for a fun trip.

But it is partly my fault. She's still pissed about the Craigslist ad.

I did take it down straight after the meeting, like I'd said I would, but it seemed some creepers had kept hold of her number and kept calling her at all hours. So, she had to get a new cell phone number.

Honestly, I feel like a bit of a shit about it now.

I tried to apologize, but those were the times when she told me to fuck off and that she hated me.

I just wish we could get back to when we were getting along, and I hadn't screwed things up with her because of the Sierra thing. And, yes, news flash—I'm taking responsibility for that. Sure, I didn't tell Sierra to come to my office to try to seduce me, but I also didn't head her off at the pass. And, if I hadn't screwed her in the first place or if I'd been honest with Morgan and told her when she hired Sierra, then it wouldn't have happened the way it did, and Morgan might still be talking to me right now.

The taxi comes to a stop at our hotel. We're staying at the Secret Garden Chiang Mai for three nights. I don't know much about the place because Chrissy booked it for us. All I know is that it's close to Ananda.

Hopefully, it has a bar, as I'm going to need a shitload of alcohol to get me through this trip.

I pay the driver, and Morgan and I get out of the car.

The heat is stifling.

The driver gets our bags out of the trunk, and a hotel porter is already loading our luggage onto a cart.

I have one small suitcase and a bag for my laptop and shit. Morgan has a large suitcase, a small suitcase, and hand luggage.

Apparently, she doesn't travel light. But I haven't commented on that fact, for fear of getting my foot stamped on again—or worse, getting kicked in the nuts.

We walk into reception and straight to the desk.

"Hi." The woman behind the desk smiles at us.

"We've got a reservation under Cross."

She taps some keys on her keyboard. "Ah, yes. Mr. Cross and Miss Stickford. Staying for three nights. Miss Stickford, you are in our Flower bungalow. Mr. Cross, you are in the Hibiscus bungalow. The bungalows are attached, so you are right next to each other."

Awesome.

"I'll just need a credit card in case you want to charge food and drinks to your room. Nothing will be charged until you check out."

I pull my company credit card from my wallet. She takes it and swipes it through a card reader, and then she hands it back to me.

"Here are the keys for your bungalows." She puts them on the counter.

I pick them up and hand Morgan hers. She doesn't say a word. Honestly, I can't remember the last time she spoke. I'm starting to wonder if her voice has stopped working, which wouldn't be an entirely bad thing.

"Also, here is a map of the hotel." The receptionist lays it out on the counter. "This is where your bungalows are." She taps to a point on the map. "Just follow the path out of here, and you'll find them, no problem. Chula has taken your luggage straight to your bungalows, so they will be there, waiting for you."

"Thanks," I say, picking up the map.

"Do the rooms have air-conditioning?" Morgan asks the receptionist.

So, her voice is still working. Shame.

"Yes. The bungalows are all fitted with air-conditioning."

"Do the bungalows have Wi-Fi?" I ask.

"Yes. You can access Wi-Fi anywhere on the hotel grounds. Here is the Wi-Fi address and password." She hands me a slip of paper, which I pocket.

"Thanks," I say.

"Enjoy your stay with us."

Yeah, I'm sure it's going to be a blast.

Morgan walks out first, and I follow behind. We walk in silence to our bungalows.

When we reach them, Morgan unlocks the door to her bungalow. She walks inside and shuts the door behind her without a word.

Okay then.

I let myself into my bungalow.

It's an open plan. Not huge, but it'll do. There are two double beds, a TV, a small kitchen area, and a separate bathroom.

My suitcase is waiting for me by one of the beds. I dump my laptop bag on the bed and lift my case up onto there, too. I open it up and get my wash bag out, and then I go take a shower.

Fresh out of the shower, I dress in shorts and a T-shirt. Then, I check my phone.

A few emails from Chrissy. Dom and Coop are arguing over an upcoming basketball game in our group message. But, apart from that, nothing of interest.

I could go get something to eat, I guess, but I ate on the plane, and I'm not that hungry. I'm not tired either.

So, what should I do?

Fuck it. I'm going to go to the bar and have a drink.

I pocket my wallet and cell and let myself out of my bungalow.

I lock the door behind me. Then, I hesitate, wondering if I should knock on Morgan's door and ask her if she wants to join me.

But then she's not exactly talking to me at the moment, and I don't relish in the thought of having her tell me to fuck off again.

So, I shove my hands into the pockets of my shorts, and I wander off in the direction of the main hotel.

I find the bar easily enough. It's right next to the outdoor swimming pool.

I take a seat on one of the barstools and order a pint of one of the local beers.

I've just taken a sip of my beer when a woman slips onto the barstool next to me, putting her purse down on the bar.

I glance at her, and she smiles.

"Hi," she says.

"Hi."

She orders a white wine, and I take a moment to look her over.

I'd say she's in her late thirties. Long red hair. Decent rack. Attractive face.

She's no Morgan. But then no one is.

Hence the situation my cock and I find ourselves in.

The bartender puts the woman's wine down in front of her, and she takes a drink. Then, she turns on her stool to face me.

"I'm Audrey." She holds her hand out to me.

I slide my hand into hers. "Wilder."

"Interesting name."

"I'm an interesting guy."

"I bet you are." She laughs softly. "So, Wilder, tell me, what brings you to San Kamphaeng?"

"Work."

"What kind of work?"

"I'm here to meet with a supplier to check out materials."

"Materials, huh? So, you work in the clothing industry?"

"Lingerie."

Something hot flashes in her eyes. "Lingerie, huh? Which brand? I might know it."

"Under Her."

"Would you believe me if I said I was wearing one of your bra and panty sets right now?"

"I wouldn't have a reason to disbelieve you," I say.

She smiles. "So, what exactly do you do at Under Her?"

"What do you think I do?"

"Well, the fact that you're here, meeting with a materials supplier...I'd say, buyer."

"CEO."

"My ex-husband's a CEO. Not for a lingerie company though."

Ex-husband. She wants me to know she's single. Meaning she's looking for a hook-up.

I can't even muster up the effort to care. Right now, all I can think about is Morgan and what she's doing back in her room and if she's even noticed I left mine.

"My divorce was finalized a week ago," she continues. "That's why I'm here, on a trip with my friend to celebrate my return to singledom."

"Where's your friend now?" I ask out of politeness.

"Oh, she's in her room—sunstroke." She laughs and rolls her eyes. "So, Wilder"—she moves closer to me, tilting her body toward mine—"I'm not usually this forward," she says in a lowered voice. "But"—she hesitates, biting her lip—"I was wondering if you'd like to…come back to my room with me."

I stare at her, waiting for something to happen in my pants.

But there's nothing.

Not even a flash of excitement at the prospect of fucking a hot divorcee, who probably hasn't had sex in a long time.

Fucking Morgan and the fucking voodoo she's put on my cock.

I hate her.

Well, I don't hate her.

The awful fucking truth is, I can't have sex with anyone else because I want Morgan.

No one else. Only her.

And I hate the fact that I can't have her.

I let out a breath. "I'm really sorry…" I say. I see a flash of disappointment flicker through her eyes. "It's not you," I'm quick to add. "You're hot. Really hot. Any other time, and I'd be grabbing your hand and leading you straight back to your room. But"—I stare down into my beer—"I just…can't."

"You don't have to explain. It's fine." She plasters on a smile and downs her drink. "Can't blame a girl for trying though, right?" She slips off her stool and picks her purse up.

"Audrey, just because I said no…don't let that put you off. What I mean is"—I rub my forehead—"the next guy you ask back to your room will be all over that…you." I force a smile. "If this were a few weeks ago and you were asking me to go back to your room, I wouldn't have hesitated. It's just…my head's a little screwed up right now."

"Yeah." She sighs. "Love will do that to you." Then, she walks away.

I want to call after her and tell her that I'm not in love with Morgan. My dick and I are just a little obsessed with her. Well, a lot obsessed.

But whatever.

Sighing, I drain my drink and leave the bar.

I take the long walk back to my bungalow.

When I get close, I see Morgan is sitting out on the terrace, reading a book. She's wearing this long black caftan, and her hair is tied up in a knot on the top of her head.

Fuck. She's beautiful.

It's weird. For the last thirteen years, I thought she was judgmental and stuck up.

But, deep down, I liked her. I just didn't like the fact that she didn't like me, and I didn't know why.

It's frustrating to have someone hate you for no reason at all. Especially when, under any other circumstances, you would have wanted to be friends with them.

Wanted more from them.

Wanted more from her.

Like I do now.

Her head lifts from her book as I approach. She doesn't look at me like she wants to kill me, so I take that as progress.

I sit down on the chair next to hers. "Can we have a cease-fire? We're in this beautiful country, and I know we're here to work, but I'd like us both to have a good time as well."

She sighs and closes her book. "Okay," she says.

My eyes flick to hers. "Okay?" I echo.

"Yeah. You're right. You did a dickish thing with the Craigslist ad, but I wasn't entirely innocent either in all of this. So, yeah, let's call a cease-fire. We have to work together, and we were getting along okay before the whole Sierra incident." Her mouth tightens around Sierra's name.

"I am sorry about that."

She doesn't say anything, and I lean back in my chair.

I risk a glance at her, and she's frowning. Her mouth still tight. Her eyes lit.

And then it dawns on me that maybe she's not pissed because I slept with her assistant. She's pissed because I didn't sleep with her.

She's jealous. And she wants me.

I know I said that to her when we were arguing—that she wanted to screw me—but I didn't actually believe it. I was trying to piss her off.

Now, I'm starting to think I was right.

There's a fine line between sex and hate. Okay, so it's love and hate. But Morgan and I don't love each other. We just want to fuck each other's brains out.

And knowing that makes the whole staying away from her a hell of a lot more difficult.

20

It's early evening, and I'm sitting in the back of a stretch limo with Morgan beside me. Niran, the owner of Ananda, and his wife, Noon, are sitting opposite us. We are on our way to watch a Thai boxing match—at the insistence of Niran.

I figured we'd probably just go out for dinner and drinks with them, but apparently, Thai boxing is the thing to do here.

Should be interesting.

Morgan and I went to Ananda today and spent the day looking around the factory and meeting with Niran and his staff.

I learned a few things today. Apparently, Morgan can speak Thai—hot as fuck. Even though Niran can speak fluent English, Morgan would at times speak to him in his native language. I got a semi from just listening to her speak.

I also learned that Ananda had some great fucking silk. Better than our Chinese supplier to be brutally honest.

I'm surprised no other company has swooped in and bought up all their stock. But I'm also really fucking glad they haven't.

I was really impressed while walking around the factory. It was a larger setup than I had expected. And the materials were of incredible quality. Seeing it all, watching Morgan's face light up at the prospect of her idea coming to life, was quite simply fucking awesome.

I slide a glance at Morgan.

She's looking extra fuckable tonight.

She has on a sleeveless white dress. Low cut in the bust and shorter on the legs than I've ever seen her wear. I'm guessing it's because of the heat here. Thank you, Thailand. So, she's showing plenty of those golden pins. I'm finding it hard not to spend the whole car journey just staring at her legs.

I keep imagining them wrapped around my waist while I fuck her.

She's wearing flat sandals on her feet, which is different, too, because Morgan is always in heels in the office. She looks so much smaller with the flats. She's not particularly short for a woman. I'd say she's about five-seven or five-eight. But I'm six-three, so she's a hell of a lot smaller than I am.

I stare at her feet. She even has pretty feet. Her toenails are painted pink, and there's a toe ring on her second toe.

I want to take those sandals off her feet. Kiss my way up her instep and up her leg, right up to the apex of her thigh, push her panties to the side, and lick a path up her pussy.

And, now, I'm hard. I shift in the seat, moving my leg to hide my stiffy, as I think about the silkworms and pupa that Niran showed us today, which they use to make the silk. He even had me touch them.

Fucking gross.

But thinking of that does the trick, and my cock is down again, which is good, as we've reached the Phichit Boxing Stadium. Well, I say *stadium*, but it looks more like a bar or a seedy strip joint from the outside. It's just on the main street, nestled in between bars and restaurants. The entrance is open, and a guy is sitting on a stool.

The driver opens the door for us. Niran gestures for me to get out first, so I do. I climb out the car, and then I hold a hand out to help Morgan out. She takes it, and I curl my fingers around her hand, loving the feel of her soft skin, imagining how it would feel around my cock.

I hate to let her go, but I have to. I don't want to weird her out by keeping hold of her hand. I have to take things slow with Morgan. Show her what an awesome guy I really am. We're only just back on even footing, and I don't want to fuck things up by rushing it.

Niran gets out of the car, helps his wife out, and then walks over to the guy on the stool.

They shake hands and exchange words, and then Niran gives him some money.

He gestures for us to follow him inside.

This place looks shady as fuck. I put a protective hand on Morgan's lower back as we start to walk inside. She shivers under my touch. I hold back my smile.

"I don't have a good feeling about this place," I whisper to Morgan as Niran and Noon walk on ahead.

"It's fine."

"You say that now. You won't be saying that when we get murdered."

Amused, innocent eyes flicker up to mine. "Stop being a pussy, Wilder. We're not going to get murdered in here."

"Hey! I'm not a pussy. I'm all man, I'll have you know. Total badass." I have the urge to flex my muscles to show her just how tough I am.

"Sure you are, Cross." She pats my chest with her hand.

Niran is holding open the door to the arena as we approach.

Morgan leans close to my ear and whispers, "Do you want me to go in first, check out the place, and make sure no murderers are in there, waiting to kill you?"

I lean back and look into her laughing eyes. "You're hilarious," I mutter. I move past her, going through the door first.

The sound of her tinkling laughter behind me lights me up inside.

I step inside the arena, which is just basically a large room with a boxing ring in the middle, surrounded by rows of tables with seating, and a bar around the edges.

"I got a table close to the front for us," Niran tells me.

Morgan and I follow Niran and Noon over to our table. Noon sits first, Morgan takes the seat next to her, then I sit next to Morgan, and Niran takes the seat next to me.

Niran pulls out a pack of cigarettes. "You smoke?" He offers me one.

"No."

"You mind if I do?"

"Not at all."

I hate smoking. Fucking detest it. But plenty of people are already smoking in here, so I'd have just looked like an ass if I'd said I had a problem with him smoking.

"Morgan?" He offers a cigarette to her, and she declines.

Niran passes the cigarette pack down to his wife, and each of them lights one up.

A waitress appears to take our drink orders.

I order a Heineken, and Morgan orders her usual of vodka, soda, and lime. Niran orders a beer, like me, and Noon orders a glass of wine.

Noon and Morgan are chatting away, so I make conversation with Niran while we wait for our drinks to arrive.

"So, tell me about the rules of Thai boxing," I say to Niran.

"Okay, so Muay Thai, as we call it here, is known as the art of eight limbs because hands, elbows, knees, and legs can be used to attack your opponent. So, there is the Chok technique, which is punching. Sok, which uses the elbows."

"You can use your elbows in Thai boxing?"

"Yes." He nods, smiling.

"Sounds brutal."

"The fighters are well trained. Train every day. And they fight once a week. But most professional boxers retire early."

I nod in understanding. Basically, they get the shit kicked out of them on the regular, so their bodies are fucked up at a young age.

Sounds fun.

"Okay, so where was I? Oh, yes, next there is Te, which involves kicking. That's one of the most used fight actions in Muay Thai. Also, Thip, which is a foot-thrust, and Chap Kho, which is clinch and neck-wrestling."

"So, basically, they just get in the ring and beat the hell out of each other?"

"Yes." He chuckles. "But it is also an art form. Very entertaining to watch. You will like it."

"I'm sure I will."

The waitress comes over with our drinks.

I glance at Morgan, and she meets my eyes with a smile.

"Oh, the first fight is about to begin." Niran claps his hands.

I watch as two pint-sized guys get into the ring.

"So, who are we cheering for?" I ask Niran.

"Sot Ponlid. He is the one on the right."

"He is our favorite boxer," Noon tells me.

"Okay. So…go Sot." I give an encouraging fist pump.

Morgan laughs at me. "You're such a dork."

"No. I'm badass. We've already talked about this."

I grin at her, and she laughs again. My whole body warms. But not in a sexual way. I don't know how to describe it. All I do know is, I've discovered that I love making her laugh.

Morgan's laughter is awesome. She laughs without abandon, and the sound is contagious.

Making her laugh is my new favorite thing to do.

But I'm sure, when I get her flat on her back and under me, a whole host of other things will become my new favorite things to do to Morgan.

21

Niran and Noon have just dropped us off back at our hotel, and Morgan and I are walking through the gardens, toward our bungalows.

We're going to meet with Niran tomorrow morning at the factory to sign some papers, and then we'll have the rest of the day free before we fly home the next morning.

"You fancy a beer?" I ask Morgan as we near our bungalows. "I have some in the fridge in my room."

Honestly, I'm just thinking up ways to spend a little more time with her. I'm not ready for the night to be over just yet.

"Sure." She smiles. "You mind if I just grab a shower first though? I want to wash the smoke out of my hair."

I'm tempted to ask if she wants me to join her. But I don't.

Slow. Slow, Cross.

"Yeah, I think I'll grab a shower, too. Niran and Noon are great, but fuck can they smoke." I chuckle.

She laughs. "I'm pretty sure they went through a full pack each while we were at the boxing match."

"And another pack while we had dinner."

We all grabbed some food at a Thai restaurant after the boxing match.

"I actually didn't know someone could smoke while eating their food."

Morgan snickers. "I'll be about fifteen minutes." She steps into her room.

"Take your time."

I let myself in my room, strip off my smoky clothes, and climb in the shower.

I'm done in five minutes. I dress in gray pajama pants and grab two beers from the fridge. I open them up and head out onto the terrace.

I'm catching up on messages when Morgan appears.

"Hey." She smiles.

Holy fuck.

She's makeup free, not that she wears much anyway, and her hair is down and damp around her shoulders. But those aren't the reasons that I've suddenly lost the ability to speak.

No, it's the black silk cami pajama top and shorts that she's wearing. And also the fact that I know she's not wearing a bra beneath it because I can see her perky nipples poking at the fabric.

Is she trying to kill me?

If she is, what a fucking way to go though.

It takes me a full minute to find my voice. "Hi," I croak as I hand her a beer.

She sits on the chair beside me and curls her legs up beneath her.

I want her so bad. I can feel myself starting to sweat, and my heart is thudding in my chest.

I take a long pull on my beer, trying to calm myself down.

Under HER

Chill, Cross. For fuck's sake, you're acting like you've never seen a hot woman before.

But I haven't seen her before. Not like this.

"That's one of ours, right?" I point to her pajama set. Why the hell I'm reminding myself of what she's wearing, I'll never know.

"It is." She smiles around the mouth of her beer bottle before taking a drink.

Those lips around that bottle…I bet she gives amazing head.

"I know my stuff," I say.

"I know my stuff."

Jesus H. Christ.

Next time I see Coop and Dom, I'm going to have them take turns in punching me in the face for all the stupid shit that I've said to her.

I take another drink of my beer and silently berate myself for being a moronic prick.

"So, tonight was fun," she says.

"Yeah, it was." I smile at her.

"And we didn't get murdered at the arena, so that was a bonus." A slow grin slides onto her face.

I chuckle and shake my head at her. "Did you not go to a Thai boxing match the last time you were here?" I ask her.

She shakes her head. "I didn't get much time to do anything, except work, the last time I was here. I was only in San Kamphaeng for a day, as I had to visit a few more places."

"So, you didn't get to do much sightseeing?"

"Nope."

"Do you wanna go sightseeing with me tomorrow after we finish up signing the contracts with Niran?"

"Sure." She smiles. "That sounds nice."

I take another sip of my beer, happy at the thought of spending the day with her tomorrow.

"I'm surprised you haven't been out here before," she says, her voice gentle in the night air. "I'd have thought traveling was your thing."

I slide my eyes to her. "Because I'm rich?"

She shrugs but doesn't elaborate.

"I've been abroad for work—China, India, places like that. Never here though. I did go to Cabo with the boys a few times for spring break." I smile at the memories. "But, honestly, I haven't taken a vacation since…God, two years ago when Coop booked us a spontaneous trip to Vegas. I'm kinda married to my job if you haven't noticed."

"I've noticed," she says softly.

I like that she's realized how hard I actually do work.

"So, how is Cooper?" she asks me.

"He's good. Bumming around, living off his trust fund." I chuckle, and she laughs.

"You were close with Dominic Anderson as well, right? I worked with him at Starbucks," she explains.

For some reason, I don't tell her that I already knew that. "Yeah, I see him all the time. Dom's one of my best friends."

"How's he doing? I heard that he'd set up a dating app or something when he left college."

"Yeah, he created Cas-U-Safe," I tell her.

Basically, Cas-U-Safe is a dating app that people can join, so they can meet and hook up with people, and there's no risk to their safety at all. The sign-up is rigorous, and it does all kinds of background checks on people. If you pass the checks, then you're allowed a membership. Once in, you are able to browse photos of people but no details. If you see someone you want to hook up with, you send the person a message. If he or she wants to meet with you, then a date is arranged through Cas-U-Safe. The first date is held at the building they own, which has security. The first building was in Chicago. Now, they're all over the fucking world.

Under HER

The Cas-U-Safe buildings are a lot like hotels. They have a reception area, restaurant, café, cinema, bowling alley, and shit like that where the dates are held. The hotel is littered with security guards. CCTV is in all the dating areas. For an extra cost, there are hotel rooms upstairs for people to check in and fuck if they want. And a panic button is in each room. If they don't want a room, then they go on their way after having a date that was safe for them, and they can go fuck at home if they want.

The joining fee is higher than the usual dating apps, but with all the creepers in the world right now, people want to know they're meeting exactly whom they think they should be meeting and that they'll be safe. And that's what Dom's company provides for them.

"Wow. I can't believe he created Cas-U-Safe."

"Yep. Dom's one smart fucker." I don't tell her the reason he created the app though. Only Coop and I know that.

"Well, he must be doing *really* well for himself."

"Yeah, he is." I smile at my friend's good fortune.

"It's one of the biggest dating apps around," she muses.

"Number two in the world. Have you ever used it?" I ask her.

"No! Of course not." Her defensive words and tone tell me that she has.

I feel a flash of jealousy at the thought of Morgan going on a date and possibly fucking some dickhead at the building that my buddy owns.

I grit my teeth, my hand tightening around my beer bottle.

When I feel a little calmer, I say, "What about you? You still friends with those girls you hung out with at Northwestern…" I click my fingers, trying to remember their names.

"Joely. And Hannah," she says.

"Yeah, right. Joely was the one with short, dark hair, right?"

"Yeah."

"And Hannah…did she have blonde hair?"

"No. Red."

"Close." I chuckle.

But she doesn't laugh back. So, I look at her, and it's like a dark cloud has settled over her once-serene face.

Surely, she's not pissed because I didn't remember her friend Hannah properly.

"Do you still see them?" I ask.

"Joely. But not Hannah." She stands abruptly, yanking my eyes up with her. "I'm gonna go to bed."

"Oh. Right. Okay." I get to my feet.

"Thanks for the beer." She doesn't look at me.

And the good feeling that I've had all night disintegrates.

"Anytime," I say.

"Well"—she takes a step away from me, her voice sounding stiff—"good night, Wilder."

"Sleep well," I tell her.

I watch her walk back into her bungalow, the door closing behind her, shutting me out. And I stand here, confused as to how me not remembering the color of her friend's hair could piss her off so much.

Morgan
Twelve Years Ago

I'm back for my second year at Northwestern.

I spent the summer at home, working for Starbucks there. I was lucky to get a transfer, and I took on a second job at the place where my mom worked, helping reception.

It was good to be home and spend some quality time with my parents. And, of course, Joely was home, too, so we got to hang out, one-on-one, which hadn't happened in a while.

Not that I don't like Joely's roommate, Hannah, because I really do. She's lovely. We're all rooming together this year. We've got an apartment close to campus. But, growing up, it's always been me and Joely, so it was awesome for it to just be me and her.

And, honestly, I think the break away has done me a world of good.

I'm actually over my crush on Wilder.

I know, right? About freaking time.

So, now that I'm not crushing on Wilder, I don't have to pretend to not have said crush on him; therefore, I don't need to act like I think he's the biggest jerk to ever walk the face of the planet so that he doesn't know I have—sorry, *had* feelings for him. And, also, I'm over the whole him implying that I was fat.

I've decided, from now on, I'll be nice to him.

Not that I've been particularly awful to him. I've just not been *friendly* to him in the past.

But this year is going to be different. A brand-new year, and I resolve to be nice to Wilder Cross. Maybe even be friends with him.

Another change that Joely and I agreed on for this year is that we'll both have more of a social life. Joely's not here on a scholarship, like me. Her parents are a little better off than mine, and they pay her tuition and boarding fees, but she still has to work to earn money to live on.

So, it's fair to say that we both neglected our social lives last year.

This year is going to be different.

I'm actually considering maybe dipping my toe in the dating pool.

I'm nineteen years old and at college. Having fun and dating boys is a rite of passage.

Hence why I find myself at this party of some guy I don't know, but he is in Hannah's creative writing class.

The house is packed with people. Some, I recognize from classes, but a lot of them, I don't know.

Hannah disappeared the moment we got here to go talk to some people she knew. So, it's just Joely and me, standing around, people-watching.

"We suck at this," she says into my ear over the loud music.

"Suck at what?" I say back to her.

"Socializing. We've been here for thirty minutes, and we haven't talked to anyone but each other. We haven't even had a drink yet."

I chuckle. "You're right. We do suck at it. How about I go locate us a drink, and you go talk to that cute guy who's been staring at you for the last five minutes?"

"Who? Where?" Her head whips around to me.

"Straight ahead. Blue shirt. Blond hair. Super cute."

She glances over at him. He's still staring at her. He smiles at her and then starts to walk toward us.

"What do I do?" she says to me, panicked.

"Talk to him," I say, giving her a little shove forward. "I'll be back soon with drinks for us."

Just as the cute guy reaches her, I disappear and go off in search of alcohol.

I head to where I think the kitchen might be. I'm just about to push the door open but pause when I hear my name mentioned.

"Hey, did you see that Morgan Stickford's here?"

I know the voice, but I'm struggling to place it.

"I thought she'd didn't do parties."

"She doesn't usually," another male voice says.

"I'm thinking I might give her a try tonight," the first voice says.

Oh, wow. Some guy is saying that he wants to hit on me. Even if he's not my type, it's still really nice to hear that I've caught a guy's interest.

A voice laughs. "Hartwell's going for the fatty again tonight to ensure he gets his dick wet."

Fatty.

I take in a sharp breath. Instant tears prick at my eyes. I suck them back.

"You mock, but the fat ones always give it up easier. They're so fucking desperate for attention, they'll spread their legs at the click of a finger."

Dean Hartwell.

He was in my economics class last year. Seemed like a nice guy. Clearly, he's not.

I wrap my arms over my chest, my insides trembling with hurt.

Don't cry. Don't cry.

I was feeling so good about myself earlier. But now...

I glance down at the dress I'm wearing, and all I can see are lumps and bumps.

I pull at the fabric to loosen it. To try and hide what I forgot for a while was there.

Fat.

I want to go home.

And then do what? Eat? Cry?

Well, it would be a hell of a lot better than standing here, listening to a bunch of guys calling me fat.

I step away from the door. But...if I leave, Joely will want to come with me. And I don't want to spoil her night. Not now that she's met some guy she might like.

For Joely's sake, I just need to suck it up and go in there to get our beers.

They probably won't even notice me anyway.

I take a few hundred deep breaths. Then, I gingerly push the kitchen door open.

The sound of male laughter assaults my ears. At first, I think they're laughing at me again, but with one quick glance, I see they're not even looking my way.

As my eyes pull away, I catch sight of Wilder, and my heart bangs painfully against my chest.

He's in the group. Standing with those guys who were just calling me fat.

He's leaning against the kitchen counter, his eyes down, focused on his cell phone.

"You've been on your phone since you fucking got here," one of the guys says to Wilder. "What—or should I say, *who* has got you so interested?"

"No one."

Wilder goes to pocket his cell, but the guy snatches it before he can.

"Holy fucking shit!" the guy crows. "Cross is getting titty pics from some chick!"

"What? Let me see!" Hartwell makes a grab for the phone.

But the guy holding it moves it out of his way, and instead, he turns the screen around for everyone to see.

Me included.

Even from my spot at the other side of the kitchen, I can see the picture. It's a nude. Well, she's wearing panties but nothing on top, her large breasts on show.

My heart sinks to my feet.

Wilder was standing there, sexting with some girl who liked to send nudes, while those guys were calling me fat, and he said nothing.

But then I shouldn't expect anything else from him. Because he is one of those guys.

"*Shiiit*! That is one impressive fucking rack!" one of them hoots.

Wilder jabs the guy holding the phone in the stomach, and as the guy bends over from the hit, Wilder grabs his phone from his hand.

"Fucking pricks," Wilder grunts.

"Hey, Cross, you should send that pic to Hartwell. He needs it more than you do. He can jerk to it when he's home alone later."

At the mention of Dean's name, I put my head down and make a beeline for the keg.

I'm just filling up my second cup of beer when I hear my name.

I freeze. Then, I look up.

Dean Hartwell is standing right near me. A beer in his hand.

My eyes flicker to the group of guys he's with. They're all talking. Wilder is back on his phone. I look back to Dean.

"Hey, Dean," I say quietly.

The cup is full, so I flip the lever on the keg, pick my other beer up, and turn to leave, but Dean stops me.

"Hey, where you going?"

"Drinks. I have to take my friend her drink."

"Stay. Chat with me for a bit."

I bite the inside of my cheek. I always do that when I'm nervous.

My eyes flicker to the group. Wilder's still on his phone.

"So, how was your summer?" Dean asks me.

"It was good, thanks."

"Cool. Mine, too. I spent it in Europe with my family."

"Sounds nice," I say because I don't know what else to say. I just know that I want to get out of here and back to Joely.

"Yeah, it was great," he says. Then, he takes a step closer.

I suck in a breath and fight the urge to run, as I don't want to give them another reason to laugh at me.

"So"—Dean reaches up and tucks some of my hair behind my ear, and I shudder on the inside—"I thought about you a lot over the summer."

His lips lift at the corners into what I'm sure he thinks is a sexy smile. All it does is make me feel sick.

"Um, you did?" I don't know what else to say. I know where he's going with this, but I just want to get out of here as fast as possible.

Dean chuckles a low sound. "Because I like you, Morgan. And I was thinking"—he moves even closer—"that we should go upstairs and get to know each other a little better."

"I, uh…" I'm sliding along the counter, beer in each hand, edging away. "I can't. I, uh, I have to get back to my friend."

His body turns, following mine. "I'm sure she wouldn't mind if you didn't go back straightaway."

"No. I, um…I have to…get her drink to her." I spin on my heel, sloshing beer over my hands, but I don't stop. I get the hell out of that kitchen as soon as possible.

As the door shuts behind me, raucous laughter breaks out in the kitchen.

"Struck out with the fatty!" One of them laughs. "Looks like you're gonna need that titty pic of Cross's after all!"

And I die a little more on the inside.

I'm getting drunk.

I know, I know. I'm being stereotypical. A bunch of guys called me fat, and I'm getting drunk.

But, honestly, the more I drink, the less my insides hurt. So, drinking, it is.

Joely knew something was wrong when I came back from the kitchen, but I told her that I was fine. I know Joely. She would have gone and given Dean a piece of her mind. Then, she'd have suggested we leave the party and go grab some pizza, meaning she'd have left behind the cute guy who was clearly into her.

So, I smiled and told her I was fine and that she should go dance with the cute guy, who I now know is called

Todd. It took a few times of persuading her until she finally relented.

So, while she's been dancing with Todd, I've been knocking back the drinks. Well, I've only had three beers, but I'm a cheap date.

And a fat one apparently.

Can anyone say *bitter*?

Okay, so I'm super drunk now.

I'm on my…fifth beer. I think. It could be sixth. Who knows? All I know is, I'm buzzing, and I feel awesome!

Joely is currently on the sofa, making out with Todd, and I'm super happy for her.

Really, I am. I love Joely, and I want her to be happy.

And at least one of us is getting some.

She didn't just leave me standing here alone though. She kept coming to check on me every so often. I told her I was going to leave the party if she came to check on me one more time. She got the hint and hit the sofa with Todd, and she's been sucking face with him since.

I've not been standing here like a sad loner though. Hannah came to chat for a bit, and then she vanished again. I was talking to Andrea from my business enterprise class until her boyfriend turned up, and she disappeared off with him.

I laugh to myself, like the loser that I am.

My bladder squeezes.

Ugh, I need to pee. I haven't been to the bathroom all night, and I've drunk about a gallon of beer. It's surprising that my bladder hasn't burst already.

I take the stairs, dodging the people sitting on them.

When I reach the landing, I walk down the hallway. There are, like, a hundred doors here.

Okay, not a hundred, but enough. And not one has a sign saying, *Bathroom Here*.

The last thing I want to do is walk into someone's bedroom and see people going at it.

I pick a door and step close to it. I lean in, seeing if I can hear anything. There's no noise, so I try the door. It opens, and no one is in there, but it's a bedroom.

I shut the door and step close to the next door.

"Fuck yes! Right there, Benji! Right there!"

Benji?

My next-door neighbor back home has a dog called Benji. He's a poodle.

And, now, I'm imagining that the Benji behind the door has hair like a poodle.

I snort and cover my mouth to catch the sound.

Yeppers, I'm totally drunk.

I stumble away from the door, chuckling to myself, and bump into the wall.

"Oh God, Wilder. You're so good at that."

I stiffen at the sound of the breathy female voice.

My head turns to the door next to me. It's a little ajar, so I can hear them but not see them.

"You like that, huh?"

"God, yes," she moans softly.

And I close my eyes against the hurt spilling into my chest.

Because I know that voice. Her voice.

Hannah.

"You're gonna make me come," Hannah whispers.

"That's what I'm aiming for." Wilder chuckles, deep and low.

She moans louder this time.

Then, there's silence. The rustling of clothes.

I need to leave.

I'm standing out here, like a creeper. Someone could come out and see me. But I just can't seem to make myself move. The betrayal is just too much.

"Wilder, you, um...you won't tell Morgan what we just did, will you?"

"Morgan?"

"Morgan Stickford. She's in some of your classes, same major."

"I know who Morgan is. I'm just wondering why you think I'd tell her that you and I hooked up. We're not exactly friends."

"No, but she's, um...well, she's kind of a friend of mine."

Kind of a friend? Nice, Hannah.

"And she, um...well, she..."

Don't do it, Hannah. Don't you fucking tell him.

"Well...she kind of...likes you."

Wilder laughs loudly. The sound splinters into my chest.

"Morgan doesn't like me." He laughs again. "She can't fucking stand me."

"Yeah, yeah, you're right," Hannah says quickly. "I was thinking of someone else. I just can't believe she doesn't like you."

Silence.

"I like you," she says in that breathy voice again.

"Well, babe"—his voice sounds rough, raspy—"why don't you get down on your knees and show me exactly *how* much you like me?"

Finally, my legs move. I stumble away, quickly heading for the stairs.

I rush out of the party. I don't wait to tell Joely that I'm leaving. She'd know something was wrong, and I really don't want to tell her what just happened. Because I know she'll be furious with Hannah, and I don't want to be the reason that they fall out. Also, we have to live with Hannah for the next year.

God, I have to live with Hannah for the next year.
What if she starts dating Wilder?

I shut my eyes and take a deep breath. I don't want to think of that right now. I'll deal with it if and when the time comes.

I pull my cell from my pocket and call for a cab. Then, I text Joely to say that I'm not feeling well and that I'm heading home.

I walk a little ways down the street, away from the party, and lean back against a wall of a neighboring house.

"Morgan doesn't like me. She can't fucking stand me."

The sound of Wilder's words and his laughter ricochet through my mind.

He thinks I don't like him. He should think that because that's what I spent the last year ensuring he would think.

And I was right to do so. Because he's an asshole.

Hating Wilder is the only line of defense that I have left now.

Because I've been lying to myself for a long time.

I don't have a crush on Wilder.

I'm in love with him.

And loving someone like Wilder Cross is pointless and a surefire way to get a broken heart for a girl like me.

If he hasn't broken it already.

23

Morgan and I spent a few hours at the factory this morning with Niran, going over a few final details and signing some paperwork, and then we were done. Afterward, he insisted we use his driver for the rest of the day to go sightseeing.

So, Morgan and I are in Niran's limousine with plenty of time for sightseeing.

That means, I get Morgan all to myself for the rest of the day.

She's seemingly back to normal today after her weird moment last night.

Seriously though, I do not understand women at all. They get bent out of shape over the smallest of things.

But then it's not Morgan's head that I want to get into. I just want in her panties.

Charmer—that, I am.

And my plan today is to show her what a fucking awesome guy I really am, and then after spending all day around my awesomeness, Morgan will realize that she needs to be fucked by me immediately. She'll drag me back to the hotel, and we'll screw each other's brains out all night long.

It's a simple plan. But, sometimes, simple is all you need for an effective outcome.

And I really hope my out*cum* is *in* Morgan, or I swear to God, I will lose my ever-loving mind. I will quite possibly need to be committed to a mental institution due to insanity caused by lack of sexual activity, and I'll also have to face my cock shriveling up and dying from lack of pussy stimulation.

I shudder at the thought. So, if I want to keep my cock alive, it is vital that he finds his way into Morgan's wet and willing pussy today.

Sometimes, women need to be romanced to get their juices flowing. And I'm not the most romantic of guys, but Niran recommended that we go visit the San Kamphaeng Hot Springs as one of our sightseeing spots today.

I figure, what better place to get Morgan hot…than at a hot springs?

Okay, that sounds fucking terrible, even to my own ears.

What the hell is wrong with me?

Since Morgan came back into my life, I've turned into a fucking dimwit.

I really need to get back on my game; otherwise, I'm going to be draining the vein via the five-knuckle shuffle tonight. Before being committed to an insane asylum, minus a working cock.

Sound dramatic? Well, try being me these past few weeks, unable to fuck any other women, and the only woman I actually want to fuck has been unavailable to me. Then, try telling me I'm being dramatic.

Okay, so moving on.

"You're surprisingly quiet," Morgan says from beside me.

Under HER

"Sorry. I was just thinking about work." *Sure you were, Cross. If business is how you're going to get into Morgan's panties.*

"Anything I need to know about?"

There's a hint of concern in her voice, so I reassure her, "No, nothing major. Just some stuff I have to do when we get back home."

"Well," she says, turning her body to mine, "I say, don't think about work now. Think about that when we're home. We're in Thailand. And we have the whole day to explore." She grins.

Her smile infects me, tilting my lips up. "You're right. No more work. Just fun for the rest of the day, babe."

Something hot and smoky flashes through her eyes.

She likes that I called her babe.

Interesting.

Maybe Morgan and I are more of similar minds than I realized.

The let's-get-naked-and-fuck kind of minds.

Jesus, I'm so fucking tempted to jump her right now.

But I hold back.

She's been looking forward to going sightseeing, and she deserves to have some fun after all the hard work she's put in with the Ananda deal.

So, I'll hold off for as long as possible before I stick my moves on her. And then stick it in her.

God, I'm such a romantic.

Our driver pulls the limo up outside the Hot Springs. I tell him to wait for us, and then Morgan and I exit the vehicle.

Morgan and I argue over who's paying the entry fee. In the end, I lie and tell her that I'm charging it to the company, but I pay it myself. It's the only way she'd let me pay.

Then, we're inside and walking around.

Basically, it's just warm water spurting out of the ground and some pools of water set in gardens. But Morgan seems to like it. And I'm happy if she is.

"It's so pretty," she says softly beside me, trailing her fingers through the pool of water we've stopped by.

"Yeah," I say. *But not as pretty as you.*

We walk on a little farther and see people are taking off their shoes and walking into the water from the springs.

"You wanna?" I gesture to the barefoot people in the water, walking around, looking like they're enjoying themselves.

"Yeah." She smiles, and it nearly blinds me.

We slip our shoes off. Thankfully, I'm wearing shorts, and Morgan has a knee-length skirt on, which she hitches up a little as we step into the water.

It's nice. Warm. Like bath water.

I feel water hit the backs of my legs, and I see Morgan grinning.

I turn to her. "Did you just kick water at me, Stickford?"

"Maybe." Her brow lifts in challenge.

"Right. That's it." I charge for her. Sweeping her up off her feet, I fling her over my shoulder.

She screams with laughter. "Put me down, Wilder!"

"You really want me to put you down?" I lean forward with her, holding on to her with my hand on the backs of her legs.

"You're gonna drop me!" she squeals, banging her hands on my back.

"Am I?"

Then, I surge forward, like I'm going to drop her in the water, and she screams.

"Wilder! Don't you dare!"

"Say you're sorry for kicking water at me."

"What? No way!"

"Okay. A soaking, it is."

"No! Okay, I'm sorry for kicking water at you!"

"And say, *Wilder, you're so awesome. I'm so sorry for thinking you were a dick for all those years.*"

"I'm not saying that!"

I feel her huff of anger against my back, and I have to hold back my laughter.

"Okay then…" I lunge with her again, and it works.

"Okay! I was wrong! You weren't a dick in college, and you're not a dick now!"

"See? That wasn't too hard, was it?"

Grinning, I slide her down my body until she lands on her feet in the water, enjoying the feel of her against me.

I expect her to move away, but she doesn't. Fiery eyes stare up at me. A thrill shoots through my body.

"You're a jerk," she says, but she's smiling.

"You really want me to toss your ass in this water, don't you?"

Her eyes narrow on me, and I let out a laugh.

"God, you're fucking adorable when you're mad."

"I'm not adorable." She pokes me in the chest with her finger. "And I can't believe you just forced me to say you weren't a dick in college. Just so you know, I take it back. You were a dick."

I catch hold of her finger, wrapping mine around it, keeping her there with me. "I know, at times, I was. And I know we didn't get along in college," I say gently. "But I always thought you were smart and tenacious."

"Sure you did." She rolls her eyes, turning her face away from me.

I know I'm losing her, so I catch her chin in my hand, forcing her focus back to me. I want her to listen to me. I want her to *hear* what I'm saying.

I know I said I wanted her in my bed. I still do. But I'm not telling her this to make that happen, I realize. I'm telling her because it's the truth, and I want her to know that.

"I thought you were strong and smart, and I admired that about you. I still do. You worked your ass off in college. You never strayed from your goals. And look where you are today. No one gave this to you. You earned everything you have right now."

I have her attention now. She's staring at me, rapt.

I brush my thumb over her skin, and her breath catches.

My eyes dip to her lips and then back to her eyes. "I think you're incredible. I like how you don't take my bullshit. You never did."

The fire in her eyes turns into something else. Something that I really, really like the look of.

"I like you, Morgan." *So fucking much.*

I inch my mouth in closer to hers. I can feel her warm breath on my lips.

Her eyes flutter shut.

I'm so close to kissing her that I can almost taste it. Taste her.

God, I want her. I've never wanted anyone like I want Morgan.

And I'm just about to erase the last of the space between our mouths and finally kiss her after all this time when the shrill scream of a young girl getting soaked by the shooting spring jolts us apart.

For fuck's sake.

The disappointment I feel is immense. But I don't let it show on my face.

"We should probably go," she says, skirting past me and out of the water. She bends over and picks up her shoes.

I follow after her. "Morgan," I firmly say her name.

She turns to me, and the look in her eyes is…almost pleading.

The words die on my tongue.

I hold back the sigh I feel. "Are you hungry?" I ask instead, bending to pick up my own shoes. "I was thinking we could grab some food before getting back on the sightseeing trail."

I see relief flicker through her eyes, and honestly, I don't know what it means. I don't know what any of this means. Because I *know* she wanted me to kiss her. I could see it in her eyes. Feel it in her body.

But I also know, if I push her now, she'll just clam up on me.

"Sure," she answers. "I could eat something."

Okay, so food first and questions later.

And there will be questions. Because, now that I know for sure she wants me, I'm not letting her get away.

24

We end up in a bar that serves local food, as we couldn't get a table at any of the restaurants we tried. But the menu looks good, and they serve beer, so it works for me.

I honestly don't care where I am so long as I'm with Morgan.

Look at me turning into a sappy fuck.

We take a table in the back. I pick up the menu and browse over it. It's all written in Thai, so Morgan translates for me.

"How come you learned Thai?" I ask her.

It's just not your conventional language. Most people in business learn Spanish or Mandarin.

She shrugs. "I speak Spanish, French, and Mandarin as well."

I stare at her, stunned. "You speak four foreign languages?"

"I'm not fully fluent in Thai. I only started learning it a few years back when I knew I would be coming here. And I guess I'm just a fast learner." She shrugs again, like it's no big deal.

"You're fucking amazing," I tell her. The words are out before I can stop them. But they are the truth.

And the way her cheeks turn pink as a shy look crosses her face tells me that I just did the right thing.

"Say something to me in all those languages."

"Nope." She shakes her head, biting down on a smile.

"Come on, Morgan." I put my elbows on the table and lean forward. "You know you want to."

Mirroring me, she puts her elbows on the table and moves in close. My breath catches at her nearness.

"No, I really don't."

"Spoilsport."

I pout, and she laughs.

"Guess I'll just have to get you drunk and try again later." I grin and sit back in my seat.

"Yeah. Good luck with that." She chuckles and then stands up. "I'm gonna use the restroom. Back in a minute."

"You want me to order for you?"

She pauses and glances down at the menu on the table. Then, she lifts her eyes to mine. "Sure. I'll have whatever you're having."

I watch her walk away, her ass swaying as she goes.

God, I need to have that ass in my hands and bury my face between those gorgeous legs of hers.

No sex thoughts, Cross.

You need to figure out what's going on in her mind before you can even get to sex.

Slow. Slow.

I get out of my chair and head over to the bar to order our food and drinks.

The bartender is busy, so I lean my elbows on the counter and wait.

"Wilder." A female voice has me turning my head.

"Audrey. Hi." I smile, shifting around to face her.

She steps a little closer to me—not invading my personal space, more like she wants to say something but doesn't want everyone to overhear.

And I'm right when she says in a quieter voice, "I was hoping I'd see you again before I left. I wanted to thank you...for turning me down the other night." She doesn't sound like she's being bitchy. She actually sounds genuine.

"Well, that's the first time a woman's ever said that to me."

I laugh, and so does she.

"Seriously though, I wasn't doing it for the right reasons, and even though you're gorgeous, I know that I would have regretted it in the morning if we had slept together."

"Well then, you're welcome."

I'm taking the glory for this, but I know me, and if I wasn't so hung up on Morgan, I would have nailed Audrey without a second thought.

And knowing that she would have walked away from that, feeling shitty, has me thinking about how many other women I have screwed who have regretted it.

And I'm not thinking in terms of a dent on my ego. But...well, I would never want a woman to leave after having sex with me, feeling like crap because she screwed me for all the wrong reasons.

Then, I think about Morgan. What if we have sex and then she regrets it afterward? Honestly, it would fucking gut me.

"How are things going with that girl who had your head all messed up?" Audrey asks, breaking into my thoughts.

"Ah. Well, nothing's changed. But I'm hoping it will soon."

She gives me an encouraging smile. "I'm sure it will. How could any girl resist you for too long?"

"True." I give a cheeky grin.

"Well, it was good seeing you again."

"You, too." I smile.

Audrey leans in and presses a kiss to my cheek. "You're a good guy, Wilder. Take care." Then, she's gone.

I stand here a moment, staring at the empty spot where Audrey just stood.

I can't stop thinking about what she said. About regret.

I never thought I had any regrets. But I do.

I regret all the time I've spent fighting with Morgan. And I don't just mean since she came back into my life. I mean, back in college, too.

Things could have been so different if we'd just pulled our heads out of our asses and actually spent time getting to know one another.

Because I'm pretty fucking sure we'd have ended up together back then if we had done that.

And I don't mean, just for a quick fuck. I mean, *together*, together.

Because that's sure as hell what I want now.

Sure, I want to bang her. I mean, Jesus, have you seen her?

But it's not just the sex. It's her.

Her smart mouth and even smarter mind. Those warm smiles and gorgeous eyes.

I want Morgan. All the time.

How the hell am I only just realizing this now?

It's not just my cock that's been obsessed with her.

All of me is obsessed with her.

My head and my heart.

I'm crazy about her.

I glance back at our table, and I see Morgan is there. But she's not sitting, waiting for me. She's on her feet, staring at me, and she looks…angry.

I push off the bar and walk over to her. "Hey, what's—"

Under HER

I don't get the rest of the words out because she slaps me so hard, the sound rings through the bar.

"Jesus Christ!" My hand goes to my stinging cheek. "What the fuck was that for?"

Livid, liquid chocolate eyes meet mine. She shakes her hand out, rubbing it with the other. "That," she says in a scary-ass, breathing-fire voice, "was for all the times you've made me feel like shit."

Then, she picks her bag up and storms out of the restaurant.

But I'm not done with her. Not by a fucking long shot.

I catch her out on the street, grabbing hold of her arm. "Oh no, you don't. You don't get to slap me and then run off. I want to know what the hell just happened."

"Why don't you just fuck off and go find your girlfriend? 'Cause I'm not interested."

"My girlfriend?" I stare at her, feeling like I've just stepped into an alternate universe. "Are you high right now?"

Her eyes narrow like lasers. And my reflexes are a little faster this time, and I catch her flying hand.

"Stop fucking hitting me," I hiss at her. "And start talking some sense to me, so I know what the fuck is going on."

She tries to free her arm from my hand, but no way am I letting go so that she can try to smack me again.

"I saw you...and the redhead. She kissed you—"

"On the cheek!"

"Clearly, you know her. And we've only been here a handful of days. So, you must know her well enough for her to feel like she can kiss you on the cheek. And knowing how you get to know women...well, I shouldn't be surprised, should I? You screwed her. Then, you sweet-talked me. *Oh, I admire you, Morgan. You never take my bullshit. I like you. Blah, blah, blah!* And I fucking believed you! Like the gullible idiot that I am.

"God, I was actually going to let you kiss me! And then you're kissing her, probably making plans to meet her later! Ugh, I'm so stupid! What were you going to do, Wilder? Try to get in my pants, and if you didn't succeed, go for round two with her? Or maybe you just planned on doing us both in the same night! Jesus! Why am I always so fucking stupid when it comes to you?"

I grab her face in my hands, forcing her to look at me. "I didn't fuck Audrey. The closest I've ever been to her was that kiss on the cheek that she gave me. I didn't kiss her; *she* kissed me."

"Well, she clearly felt comfortable kissing you," she snaps.

"She was thanking me." My voice is harsh, but I'm frustrated. She just doesn't seem to be hearing a fucking word I'm saying. "I met her at the hotel bar the first night we arrived here. She recently got divorced, she was feeling lonely, and she propositioned me."

Morgan barks out a laugh. "Of course she did. And I bet you had a lot of fun with her."

Jesus, the venom in her eyes. I've never seen her like this before.

"Just fucking listen to me for a goddamn minute!" I bark at her.

Her eyes flash with surprise, and I don't like it, but I've got her attention, so I take it and run.

"Audrey hit on me. I turned her down. She was just thanking me for turning her down because she knew that she had asked me for the wrong reasons, and she would've regretted it if we'd slept together."

"You turned her down?"

"Of course I did."

"Why?"

Is she really that blind? Does she really not see that I'm tied up in knots over her and that I have been ever since she came back into my life?

Under HER

"Because of you!" I yell, frustrated. "How the fuck could I ever want anyone else when all I think about, all I *want*, is you?"

And then I'm done talking. It's time for action.

So, I slam my mouth down on hers, and I kiss her.

25

The ride back to the hotel is a steep learning curve in the art of mastering restraint.

And, no, you kinky bastards, I'm not talking about those kinds of restraints.

I mean, restraint from screwing Morgan right here and now.

Because there is no way I'm having sex with her for the first time in the back of a limo.

Not that I've ever had a problem with having sex in a car before. But not with her. The first time with Morgan has to be perfect.

I guess I'm going soft in my Morgan-obsessed state.

But not soft in other places. My cock is currently made of steel. And I'm desperately trying not to impale her with him. But, fuck, it's difficult.

And she's not exactly making it easy for me because she's straddling my lap, her hands in my hair, tongue in my mouth, riding me through our clothes, and I'm fucking dying here.

I'm so desperate to be inside her, it's bordering on insanity.

Jesus, can this limo go any faster?

I'm half-tempted to drop the divider and offer the guy ten thousand dollars to get us back to the hotel in half the time.

But I don't want him to get a view of Morgan in her current sexed-up state.

I don't need to worry though because, a few minutes later, the limo is pulling up to a stop outside our hotel.

I don't wait for the driver to get the door. And I don't give a shit that I'm currently sporting the world's biggest boner. I open the limo door, grab hold of Morgan's hand, and drag her out of the car with me.

I all but run her through the hotel reception, toward the gardens, and in the direction of our bungalows.

I'm on a mission. And nothing and no one is going to stop me from getting inside her gorgeous body.

I'm digging in my shorts pocket for my room key as we approach the bungalows. Morgan hasn't said a word, but I can hear heavy breaths beside me, and the sound is making me even harder. Impossibly harder.

I jam the key in the door. Unlock it. Fling it open. Pull her inside. Slam the door shut and push her up against it.

Then, I just stand here and stare at her. Taking her in for a moment.

Her flushed chest is heaving up and down. Her lips are puffy from my kisses. Her eyes are laced with desire. Her gorgeous hair is ruffled.

She looks fucking beautiful.

She looks like sex.

And she's all mine.

I step up to her. Her breath catches.

"Hi," I say.

Under HER

"Hi."

She bites her lip, and I can't wait a moment longer.

My mouth crashes down on hers.

We both moan in the absolute euphoria of our kiss.

I've kissed hundreds of women. Possibly thousands. And not once have I ever felt like I do when I kiss her.

Like my whole body is on fire. Alive with the most fucking incredible sensations.

If kissing her feels like this, I can only imagine what being inside her will feel like. And the way she starts attacking my clothes, I figure I'm going to find out sooner than later.

She tugs my T-shirt up. So, I reach back, pull it over my head, and toss it to the floor. I kick off my shoes. I stick my hand in the pocket of my shorts, pull out a condom, and toss it onto the bed.

Then, I take off my shorts. Leaving only my boxers.

I've never exactly been the shy type.

I hook my thumbs in the waistband of my boxers and shove them to the floor.

Then, I meet Morgan's eyes, which are wide and fixed on my cock.

I almost come just from the look in them.

"God, Wilder..." Her eyes lift to mine. "It's so..."

"Big."

"I was going to say hard."

"It's that, too." I chuckle deep.

I step backward and sit on the edge of the bed. I lean back on my hands, and my cock juts up, large and proud. "Your turn," I tell her with a lift of my chin.

I see a flash of nerves in her eyes, but she seems to stamp it down. She meets my stare and bites that goddamn lip of hers again, like she knows it makes me crazy.

She kicks off her shoes and then takes her top off, revealing a black lacy bra.

Holy fuck, she's pretty.

Then, she unzips her skirt. The sound echoes around the room. She pushes the skirt down her hips until it's pooling on the floor, revealing her matching panties.

And it's not one of our products.

"You're wearing the competition." I tilt my head to the side.

A smile edges her lips, and she lifts her shoulder. "I like to see what I'm up against."

"Come here." I crook a finger at her.

She pads toward me. My cock pulses against my stomach, the closer she gets.

When she reaches me, I pop the clasp on her bra. Her tits spill out of them. They're more than a handful, and her nipples are rosy and perfect.

I run my finger between the valley of her breasts and down to her stomach, stopping just above the waistband of her panties.

Then, I grab hold of her hips with both hands. I catch the material of her panties with my fingers and rip it from her body. She gasps.

"Crap quality," I rasp out.

I throw the tattered panties to the floor, and my eyes drop to the spot between her legs.

She's blonde and perfect with a neat little landing strip right over the place where I'll soon be.

Taking hold of her hips again, I lift her onto the bed, so she's straddling me.

I take her face in my hands, and I kiss her.

She moans into my mouth, and I feel it all the way down to my cock.

I suck on her tongue, and the kiss turns heated, so raw and primal.

She shifts forward, and her hot, wet pussy presses against my cock.

Holy frigging hell. I practically see stars.

"I can't wait," I croak out.

"Why would you?" she gasps.

Good fucking question.

I grab the condom from the bed and tear it open. I go to put it on, but she takes the rubber from me and rolls it down onto my cock.

So goddamn sexy.

Her gorgeous eyes lift to meet mine. She has my cock in her hand.

With our eyes locked together, she slowly...so very fucking slowly sinks down onto me.

And holy sweet fucking mother of Mary. It's everything I thought it would be and more.

She's hot and tight and so goddamn perfect.

She's nirvana.

I kiss her again.

"You're so beautiful," I tell her. "So fucking beautiful."

She rises up onto her knees, almost taking me out to the tip, before sliding back down on me.

Fuck.

I keep kissing her as my hands grab her hips, urging her on.

"God, Wilder," she moans. Her head falls back, her lips parted.

She's a fucking goddess.

I dip my head and capture one of her nipples in my mouth. My finger seeks out her clit. She moans louder. Her arms come around my head, holding me to her, as she starts to ride me in short, hard strokes.

My tongue laves her nipple, and my finger rubs at her clit. Her pussy is soaked, and it squeezes my cock like a fist with each move she makes.

I'm in fucking heaven.

I can feel her body winding up like a time bomb, ready to explode. I'm close to coming myself. It's taking everything in me not to shoot my load now. She's that fucking hot. That fucking good. But I want this to last as long as possible. I want her to come before me.

In one swift move, keeping myself inside her, I flip her to her back.

"My turn," I tell her.

My body crashes to hers. I hook a hand under her leg, and I start to fuck her. Pumping in and out.

"Yes! Wilder! Harder! Fuck me harder!"

So, I do.

I slam in and out of her. Flesh slapping flesh. The best fucking sound in the world.

"Yes…God…Wilder…that's…it…" Her words fall away on a gasp. Her head rolls to the side, her eyes squeeze shut, and her body shudders as she comes around my cock, triggering my own orgasm.

"Morgan…fuck…fuck." I thrust into her, feeling mindless with sensations as I come hard and long. So hard that I'm pretty sure I black out for a second.

"Jesus," I pant, pressing my forehead to hers, running my fingers into her hair. "That was…"

"Incredible."

The best night of my life. And I've only just gotten started on the things I want to do to her.

26

I'm still inside her. I'm not ready to pull out just yet.

Morgan is gazing up at me with those inviting brown eyes of hers, a smile edging her lips.

And I just have to kiss her again. So, I do.

I brush my lips over hers.

I only intend for the kiss to be brief. But it quickly turns molten. I can't seem to get enough of her. One taste is not enough.

I wonder if anything will ever be enough with her.

Usually, when I'm with a woman, I'm getting ready to head out the door by now.

Barring the fact that I brought Morgan to my room, the only place I plan on going is down. On her.

I slip out of her body. I rise up onto my knees, remove the condom, and toss it in the trash can.

My hands land on her knees. I push her legs apart, and they spread willingly.

I run a finger through her short patch of hair and into the lips of her pussy, and she whimpers.

"You're wet for me again." I take my finger into my mouth and suck her from it.

Her lips part on a gasp, and I like that I can shock her.

Fuck, she tastes good.

Exactly like a pussy is supposed to.

I lower myself onto her body. Her pussy is wet against my abs. I take her nipple into my mouth. She cries out my name.

I spend my time alternating between her breasts, licking and sucking, until she's mindless and writhing beneath me, her hips seeking out pressure from my body.

"Wilder…I need…"

I lift my eyes to hers. "What, sweetheart? What do you need?"

There's nothing hotter than a woman telling me what she wants me to do to her. And to have Morgan tell me? Way fucking hotter.

Her eyes are lit, but there's a shimmer of embarrassment, too. I'm digging this shy side of her.

"Tell me," I rasp out. Keeping my eyes on hers, I lower my head and scrape my teeth over her nipple.

Her body shudders beneath me.

"Your mouth."

"Where?" I circle her nipple with my tongue.

"On my…pussy."

Fuck yeah.

I kiss my way down her body, settling between her legs. I run my nose between the lips of her pussy. The tiny, coarse hair tickles my skin as I breathe her scent in.

Then, I circle her clit with my tongue.

Her hips come up off the bed on a cry.

I put her legs over my shoulders and band my arm over her stomach, holding her down. I bury my face in her pussy.

Under HER

I lick and suck the most sensitive part of her body, teasing with grazes of my teeth.

When my finger pushes inside, she becomes shameless and starts riding my finger and my face.

And I fucking love it.

Her hands are gripping my hair to the point of pain, but I don't care.

My cock is rock hard again. Desperate to be where my finger is.

But he'll have to wait. I'm not fucking her until I get her where I want her to be—coming against my mouth.

I pull my finger out and push my tongue inside her, fucking her with it.

"Oh my Jesus." Her voice trembles.

I pull my tongue out and slip two fingers inside her at the exact same time as I suck her clit into my mouth.

Her body goes rigid. Her heels dig into my back. Then, she goes off like a rocket. Yelling out my name along with a bunch of obscenities.

I keep with her right until the end, until she's squirming against me.

I lift my head, wiping my mouth with the back of my hand.

Morgan looks sated, happy, lying there as she comes down from her orgasm.

For some reason, I find myself committing the image of her like this to my memory.

"That was…wow…you're really good at that." She laughs softly.

I quirk a brow. "I'm good at a lot of things."

Rising up, I lean over and grab another condom from my wallet. I slide it on. Then, I wrap my hand around my shaft and slowly jack my cock once, twice.

Her wide, lusty eyes follow the movement.

"What do you want now, Morgan?" I ask, my voice gravelly.

"You," she says.

I lean over and kiss her. She wraps her arms around my neck, bringing me closer, kissing me harder.

I easily slide inside her. She's so slick and hot and ready for me.

I go at a slow pace to begin with, and not once do I stop kissing her.

But then need takes over, and I rise up onto my hands. Staring down at her, I start thrusting harder and faster. I'm pushing her up the bed with every surge of my cock, her tits bouncing with the movement.

Her legs come up around my hips, gripping me to her. And I can't take my eyes off her.

Her hand slides up around my neck, cupping it, and she brings me back to her lips, kissing me. She sucks on my tongue, and I feel it—the heat down my spine, telling me I'm close to coming.

"Morgan…" I groan.

"Yes…that's it, Wilder…right there…"

A strangled cry leaves her lips, her legs locking tighter around me, her pussy squeezing my cock like a vise, and I explode inside her, groaning loud enough to wake the dead.

Like I give a shit.

I'm inside the most beautiful woman in the world, and I've just come inside her twice in a very short space of time.

Life is good.

No, it's fucking awesome.

27

I finally drag myself away from Morgan after another make-out session, following that last round of sex.

I'd go now again if I could, but I don't think my cock will allow it.

He needs a rest before round three.

I go into the bathroom to clean up and dispose of condom number two. I grab a washcloth to clean Morgan up with.

I catch sight of myself in the mirror over the sink.

The smile on my face is unmistakable.

It's not just an I-had-great-sex smile. It's an I-just-had-amazing-sex-with-a-woman-I've-been-craving-for-weeks-now smile.

Or maybe even longer.

I always thought she was pretty back in college. Smart and feisty. She interested me...intrigued me, I guess. And I always hated the fact that she didn't like me. That she didn't want me.

I never pursued her. Why would I have? She hated my guts. But I do know that I would have had sex with her if she'd wanted to.

But, now, I have to allow myself to think, *If we had gotten along in college, would things have been different? Would we have been together back then? Would we still have been together now?*

And, if I'm being honest with myself, I think the answer is yes to all of it.

Being with Morgan is like nothing I've ever felt before.

It's like inhaling fresh air after a lifetime of breathing smog.

I don't know what this means or what I want from her exactly. But I do know what I want at this moment in time, and it's to be with her.

I just have to hope she feels the same.

I take the washcloth back into the bedroom with me. She's sitting up against the headboard, the sheet wrapped around her.

Gotta say, I'm not liking seeing her covered up.

Reaching the bottom of the bed, I tug on the sheet, pulling it off her body.

"Much better," I say.

She smiles.

I climb onto the bed, between her legs, and she parts them for me.

I press the cloth to her pussy, cleaning her.

"You don't have to do that," she says quietly.

"I want to." I dip my head and brush a kiss to her lips. "Don't go back to your room. Stay with me tonight," I say.

She stares at me for a long moment, and then her eyes soften. "Okay," she says. "But we have to be up early to catch our flight."

I groan and climb off the bed. I toss the washcloth in the bathroom, grab my cell, set the alarm for ridiculous o'clock, and then switch off the lights.

Morgan moves down the bed, lying on her side. I climb on the bed beside her, bringing the sheet up to cover us. I pull her close, putting my arm around her. She rests her head on my chest.

"I can't believe we're here," she says quietly.

"I can."

"You can?" She lifts her head to look at me in the dark.

"Yeah." I curl my hand around her cheek, brushing my thumb over her smooth skin. "Babe, the way I wanted you…it was inevitable that you'd succumb to my charm at some point."

"Ass." She chuckles, slapping me on the chest.

"Hey, enough with the hitting, Rocky Balboa."

She bites her lip, her eyes closing. "I'm sorry…that I slapped you earlier."

"Forget it."

"No, I shouldn't have done it."

"Babe, I'm pretty sure I've deserved to be slapped on many occasions in my life. And, anyway, if you hadn't slapped me, I wouldn't have known you cared."

Her eyes open. "Who says I care?"

"I do."

"You could be wrong."

"Am I?"

Her lips press together, and I know she's not going to answer. Stubborn little thing that she is. So, I bring her mouth down to mine, stopping just short of a kiss.

"I care about you," I whisper against her lips.

Her breathing hitches. "Yeah?"

"Yeah. I care about you a fuck of a lot. And I've never wanted anyone the way I want you."

I erase the distance between our mouths, and I kiss her for the hundredth time tonight, but somehow, each time feels like the first. But this kiss isn't about sex. It's about showing her what she means to me.

And I think I'm only now just starting to realize the actual extent and depth of my feelings for her.

I'm fucking crazy about her.

I break from her lips, and both of us are panting. Her forehead presses down to mine, her hand resting against my cheek.

"It's the same for me, too, Wilder," she whispers. "Everything you said...I feel the same."

A pressure comes down on my chest, but it's a good kind of pressure. The kind of pressure that I want to feel time and time again.

Morgan moves her head to my shoulder and hooks her leg over mine. I wrap my arms around her, holding her tight to me.

And we fall asleep exactly like this.

Wrapped up in each other. Like we always should have been.

28

It's Friday evening, and we've just landed back in O'Hare after close to a day of traveling.

FYI, best frigging flight I've ever taken. Screw joining the Mile High Club. Getting Morgan off with my hand under the blanket we were sharing while people were sleeping around us and then watching her have to bite her lip to keep quiet as she came, her eyes on mine—hottest thing ever.

I can't get enough of her. I'm addicted.

When I was a kid, I went through this phase of being addicted to waffles. I had to eat them all the time—for breakfast, lunch, and dinner. I'd eat them with all kinds of different toppings and side orders. But it was the waffle I wanted.

Drove my mom crazy.

Eventually, the addiction waned.

But I still have waffles all the time. Even now. Best food ever.

Morgan is my new waffle. I want her all day, every day, in any way I can have her. And I don't ever see that ending.

We've just gotten our luggage. We have to use a cart, as, remember, Morgan doesn't travel light.

We exit the airport, head over to the taxi stand, and grab a cab.

The driver loads our luggage in the trunk, and Morgan and I climb into the back of the car.

Then, I realize that this is it. The trip is over. We'll go back to our respective apartments.

And I don't know where we stand.

We haven't talked about what this means, what's going on between us.

We were too busy screwing each other's brains out in the hotel and making out on the plane ride home to talk about the status of our relationship.

Are we in a relationship? Do I even want to be in a relationship?
I've never been in one before.

Don't judge me. I'm rich and good-looking. Why would I have tied myself to one woman when I could have them all?

But, right now…I want to be tied to Morgan. Figuratively and literally.

"I had a really good time," she says quietly beside me.

I turn my head to her. Taking her hand in mine, I lift it to my lips and press a kiss to it. "Me, too."

The driver climbs in the cab. "Where to, folks?"

I stare at Morgan, my heart pounding in my chest. "Don't go home," I blurt. "Not yet. Come back to my place."

Her eyes widen. "But…my luggage…"

"Bring it with you." I turn in my seat to face her and take her face in my hands. "Stay the weekend. I just…I'm not ready…" I can't seem to find the right words. All I know is that I'm not ready to let her go. Not yet. Maybe not ever.

A soft smile touches her lips. "I'm not ready either," she whispers.

And my chest expands with happiness. I feel like I've just won the lottery.

I have. I've won the woman lottery.

Without taking my eyes off her, I say to the driver, "East Grand Avenue and Lake Shore, please, buddy."

Then, I press my lips to hers and kiss her because I have to. Because I can.

Because she's mine.

The realization hits me like a freight truck.

Morgan is mine.

And she doesn't even know it yet. But she is, and I have no intention of ever letting her go.

Not that I'm going to kidnap her and keep her in my apartment—although that could be a good option, if she doesn't feel the same way. Kidding. Kind of.

But, for the first time in my life, I want something real. I want something with her.

I want a relationship with Morgan.

Shocker, I know.

Ladies and gentlemen, Wilder Cross no longer wants to be a hot bachelor.

I want to be a hot...I don't know. What do you call a guy in a relationship?

Boyfriend.

I want to be Morgan's hot, sexy-as-hell boyfriend.

And the thought doesn't make me break out in hives.

Well, fuck me sideways.

The more I think about this relationship business, the more I see the benefits.

As in lots and lots of sex on tap.

Sex with Morgan. Which, of course, she's fantastic at. She's amazing at everything.

Only I don't know where her head's at with it all.

I know she likes me. And she likes my cock an awful lot. But a relationship? No clue.

I could just ask her, which would be the smart and sensible thing to do.

But what if she doesn't feel the same?

What if all she wants from me is sex?

Well, shit. I didn't think of that.

She could just want me for the spectacular orgasms I provide and nothing else.

She seems to like me now, but she wasn't exactly my biggest fan in college. Deep down, she might still think I'm that same prick she thought I was in college.

I know I'm frigging awesome. But that doesn't mean she does.

Trust me, people can fuck each other without actually liking each other. All you need is sexual attraction.

How do you think Kanye got laid before he became a Kardashian?

Well, actually, that probably had a lot to do with money. Which I have in the bucketloads.

But Morgan isn't a gold digger—cue Kanye tune.

Seriously though, she's worked her ass off for everything she has. And she was never one to screw around in college. I actually don't remember her ever having a boyfriend. Thank fuck.

So, she has to like me, right? It can't just be about sex.

Okay, so now, all I have to do is spend this weekend showing her that being in a relationship with me is the best idea ever.

And I can do that.

Easy.

29

"Wow. Your place is great. This view…" Morgan walks over to the floor-to-ceiling windows, pressing her fingertips to the glass as she stares out at nighttime Chicago.

I drop our cases on the floor of my apartment and stretch out my back.

Jesus, her cases weigh a ton. I wish I'd taken the doorman's offer to help me.

My eyes focus in on her standing there, silhouette by the night, and all thoughts of heavy luggage are forgotten.

I walk toward her. My cock hardens, the closer I get to her.

Coming up behind her, I brush her hair over her shoulder and press a kiss to her neck.

"I like you here, in my apartment," I tell her.

"I like being here."

My hands drop to her hips as I trace my tongue up the skin of her neck until I reach her ear. I graze my teeth over her lobe.

She shivers.

"I want you, just like this," I whisper.

My hands push her skirt up. I shove her panties aside and dip two fingers inside her.

"God, Wilder," she moans. Her arm reaches back and curls around my neck as she turns her face to mine.

Her lips seek out mine. I part them with my tongue and plunge it into her mouth as I thrust my fingers deep inside her.

"I'm gonna fuck you right here," I tell her.

"Won't people...see?"

"Will you care if they do?" I'm slowly moving my fingers in and out of her, fucking her with them.

She stares into my eyes. "No," she finally whispers.

"Good." I brush my mouth over hers. "Now, put your palms flat against the window."

She does as I asked without question. I like it.

No, I fucking love it.

Slipping my fingers out of her, I can't resist giving her clit a teasing rub.

She moans loudly, her hips moving against my fingers, wanting more pressure.

But I pull my fingers away, and I tug her skirt and panties down to the floor.

She steps out of them. She's just about to remove her heels when I stop her.

"Keep the heels on," I growl.

She glances back at me, a sexy smile on her lips.

She's standing there, naked from the waist down, and she's the hottest thing I've ever seen.

I drop to my knees behind her and grab her ass in my hands.

Under HER

I kiss her cheek, peppering kisses lower. When I get close to my new favorite place, she tries to pull away.

"Wilder, no, I haven't showered in almost a day."

I stare up at her. "You think I give a shit? I want you. And I'm going to have you."

I spread her ass cheeks and dip my tongue inside her pussy.

She whimpers. And I start to fuck her with my tongue.

God, I love the way she tastes. The way she feels against my mouth.

My hand goes to her clit, and I start to rub at her hard nub with my fingers.

She's tight around my fingers. Her body is coiled like a spring, ready to go.

Her legs are trembling, but I don't let up.

She's panting and moaning my name over and over, and it's the hottest fucking sound ever.

When she pushes back against my face, fucking my tongue, I know she's close. When Morgan reaches that point, she's unabashed about what she wants.

She wants to come, and she'll do anything to make that happen. I fucking love that about her.

I pinch her clit. She cries out, and then her muscles stiffen, her pussy contracting around my tongue as she starts to orgasm.

I groan as she comes all over my tongue.

Hot. As. Fuck.

I get to my feet, wiping my mouth on the back of my hand.

She still has her hands against the window, her forehead tipped against it, too, as she tries to catch her breath.

But I'm not giving her a reprieve.

I get a condom from my pocket, unzip my pants, and shove them down my hips. I roll the rubber on. Grab hold of her hips. And slam inside her.

"Wilder!" she cries.

"Jesus...Morgan..." I groan, stilling inside her.

I'll never get used to how good she feels around me. Her channel is as snug as a fucking glove around my cock.

Warm and wet and mine.

Something primal tears through me, and I start fucking her hard. Pounding into her. The only sound in my apartment is the slap of our skin as we meet in each hard thrust. And the sound of our labored breaths and lust-crazed moans.

I let go of her hips and keep up the pace, my hips snapping back and forth.

I cup her tits over her shirt. Needing to feel skin-on-skin, I grab her shirt and rip it apart. Buttons scatter everywhere.

"I'll buy you a new one," I groan.

I shove the cups of her bra down and pinch her nipples with my fingers.

"God...Wilder...you're driving me crazy..."

That's what I like to fucking hear.

"You like that?"

"I like everything you do to me," she whimpers.

My balls tighten up, and desire drives down my spine.

I drop one hand to her clit and rub her slick nub with my fingers, knowing I'm getting close.

But I'm not coming without her.

She bucks back against me, meeting me thrust for thrust, as I continue to fuck her.

"Need you to come," I grind out.

"Yes...yes..." she chants. "Right...there...Wilder..."

Her pussy tightens around my cock like a fist as she comes.

"Fuck...fuck...fuck..." My hand drops from her clit, and I grab her hips and drive in and out of her like a madman. And then I'm coming, and I keep coming. And then I come some more.

Under HER

I'm pretty sure I've flooded out the condom.

"Jesus…" I gasp, my head dropping to her shoulder.

"I know," she says between breaths.

I lift my head and press a kiss to the skin below her ear. "Best sex ever," I tell her.

Unsure eyes turn to mine. "Really?"

"Yes." I kiss her lips. "Really." Kiss. "It's never been like this for me before, babe. Our sexual chemistry is off the charts, if you haven't noticed."

"I've noticed." Her teeth graze her lower lip. "This…you…it's my best ever, too."

"I'm glad to fucking hear it."

She laughs, and I kiss her again because I can't seem to stop kissing her.

"We should clean up," she murmurs against my mouth.

"Yeah, we should. I came like a motherfucker."

She laughs again. "Shower?" she suggests.

"Definitely." I reluctantly pull out of her, and then I take hold of her by her hand and lead her toward my bathroom.

30

"Fuck." My head thuds back against the wall of my shower.

Morgan is on her knees in front of me, my cock in her mouth, and she's giving me the most spectacular blow job I've ever had. And I've had a lot of blow jobs over the years.

Her hand is wrapped around the base of my cock as she bobs her head over it, her tongue swirling and licking it like it's a fucking lollipop.

"Jesus…you're so fucking good at this."

She hums around my cock, and I feel it all the way to my toes.

I can feel my orgasm approaching.

"Coming," I warn her.

I'm not a jerk. I'm not going to come in her mouth unless she wants me to.

And, apparently, she wants me to because she stays with me, her mouth around my cock, sucking me harder, as she jacks me with her hand at the same time.

And then I'm coming.

"Jesus…Morgan!" I cry out. My hand grips hold of her head, fingers tangled in her wet hair, as I shoot my load in her hot mouth.

When I'm done, she licks me clean. I stare down at her in amazement.

My limbs are like noodles. I feel boneless. And fucking awesome.

Morgan kisses her way up my body, licking droplets of water off my chest, until she reaches my mouth. "Was that okay?"

"Does the Pope shit in the woods?"

"I'll take that as a yes then."

"Take it as a big, fat yes. It was amazing, babe." I cup her face in my hands, and I kiss her.

And, no, I don't care that I just came in her mouth. I fucking love the taste of me on a woman. Even more so on Morgan. Maybe it's a primal thing.

She moans into my mouth, her hands winding into my hair, her naked body pressed to mine, and it's everything I could ever want.

We kiss for a while until we decide we should really leave the shower. We don't wash each other, as we agree it would probably end up taking a whole lot longer.

I wash my body and hair, and I'm done in three seconds flat. So, I get out and wrap a towel around my waist. I brush my teeth while Morgan finishes washing her hair.

I hear the water turn off, and I hand her a towel as she steps out of my shower.

"Thanks." She squeezes the water out of her hair and then wraps a towel around her body.

"Do you have a spare toothbrush?" she asks. "Mine's in my case, and I don't fancy digging it out."

"Sure." I get a new toothbrush out of the cupboard and hand it to her.

I leave her brushing her teeth, and I go into my bedroom and slip on some pajama pants.

Thinking about her clothes, I get her a T-shirt of mine to wear so as to save her from having to go through her case.

She appears in the doorway, sans towel, wearing nothing but a smile.

"God, you're fucking hot," I tell her.

She smiles shyly. It's so fucking awesome that she's confident enough to walk into my bedroom naked, but when I compliment her on her obvious hotness, she goes coy.

"I got you a T-shirt of mine to wear. Save you from digging through your case for clothes." I walk over and hand it to her, and of course, I kiss her because I can.

She pulls on my T-shirt. It falls to her knees.

"You hungry?" I ask her.

The last time we ate was on the plane, and that was hours ago.

"A little."

"I can order in if you want."

"Sounds great."

She follows me into the kitchen where we decide on Chinese food after looking through my many takeout menus.

I ring the order through. Then, I grab us a couple of beers, and we hit the couch.

She snuggles up into my side, and I put my arm around her.

Look at me, being all domesticated and coupley.

I used to think it would feel weird to be with a woman like this. But being here with Morgan feels as natural as breathing.

And I'm finding that I like just being with her, talking to her, spending time together as much as I like being inside her.

I pick up the remote and turn the TV on. "You wanna watch a movie?" I ask her.

"Sure. What do you have in mind?"

"We could go new or an old favorite," I say as I start to flick through Netflix. "Actually, have you seen *Breaking Bad*?" I ask as I come to a stop on it. "I know it's not a movie, but Coop has been getting on me to watch it. Apparently, it's fucking awesome."

"I've heard it's really good, too. Put it on."

I select the first episode and press play.

Then, I kick my feet up on the coffee table and take a swig of my beer.

Life really doesn't get any better than this. I have the hottest woman I've ever known in my arms after having another two amazing orgasms with her, and I have her here, in my apartment, for the whole weekend.

Nope. It definitely doesn't get any better than this.

31

I have no clue what time it is. But, by the light creeping into the sky, I'd say it's early morning.

Time seems to have no relevance while I'm here, in my apartment, with Morgan. And I should be tired after the flight. But I'm not. Not one little bit, and apparently, neither is Morgan.

We started *Breaking Bad* with the intention of just watching a few episodes. We ended up watching the whole first season. In between make-out sessions, obviously.

We had to pause the show a few times as the make-out sessions turned into sex.

Just like it did half an hour ago when the last episode finished.

So far, we've fucked on my sofa, twice, including this last time. On the kitchen counter when we washed up our plates. And the living room wall on the way back from the kitchen from washing the plates.

I'm going to have to do a condom run if we keep going at this rate.

It's amazing, how much sex we've had in such a short space of time.

I've always been the kind of guy who can go a few rounds in quick succession. But, with Morgan, I've got the fucking stamina of a stallion.

We're lying on the sofa on our sides, facing each other, a blanket covering us. Because, of course, we're both naked.

"I don't think we should get dressed for the rest of the weekend," I announce.

Smiling eyes lift to meet mine. "No?"

"Nope."

"What if we order in and one of us has to go to the door?"

"Well, you're sure as fuck not. I'm not letting some other guy see these babies." I cup her tits in my hands and squish them together.

She giggles.

"What if it's a girl delivery person? I don't want her seeing your…cock."

God, I love it when she says *cock*. She sounds so sweet, which makes the word sound even dirtier. Like when she says, *Fuck*, or, *Make me come*, or even just, *Wilder*. My name has never sounded sweeter or sexier than it does when coming from her lips.

"Okay, so if it's a dude delivering, then I'll go to the door."

"And you don't mind another guy seeing your package while he hands over his package?"

She grins, and I have to fist-bump her for that.

"Nicely put. And not at all, babe. I played sports in high school, so I'm used to showing guys my cock."

"Is this some new sport that I don't know about? Because, if it is, I want to hear all about it."

"You dirty little perv," I tease.

Under
HER

She laughs.

"I meant, in the showers. Guys aren't shy about getting naked when they have to shower together after sports. And I have a big cock, so I've no need to be shy."

"And a serious amount of confidence."

"Are you disputing the fact that I have a massive dick?"

"Never." She flashes her eyes at me. "So, am I to guess that I'm going to the door if a woman delivers the food?"

"Yep."

"Well, you might be comfortable with flashing your junk to complete strangers, but I'm not so keen on showing the girls to strange women."

"So, I'm taking it, that would also be a no to bringing the delivery girl inside, so the three of us could act out a porno fantasy of mine?"

"You ass!" she yells, shoving me in the chest.

I grab her hands, forcing her to her back, and pin them over her head. I dip my mouth to hers and kiss her. She responds immediately, moaning softly against my lips.

I fucking love how responsive she is to me.

I lift my mouth from hers and stare into her eyes. "I was kidding, babe. I'm not sharing you with anyone. Not even a hot delivery girl."

She gives me a playful scowl. I kiss her one more time and then fall back onto my side, beside her.

She turns to face me, putting her hands under her head, a thoughtful look on her face. "Have you ever had a threesome before?" she asks.

And if that isn't a loaded question.

"You really want me to answer?"

She nods.

"Yes."

She doesn't react like I thought she would. I honestly expected her to get pissed. But she still looks thoughtful.

Then, a thought occurs to me. "Have…you?"

Her lips lift at the corners. "You really want me to answer?" she tosses my words back at me.

I think for a moment. Do I want to know? Yes, if it was with another girl and guy. No, if it was with two dudes.

I don't know why, but the thought of Morgan with two guys makes me want to punch a hole in my wall.

"Okay, just answer me this...hypothetically, if you did have a threesome...how many vaginas attended this party for three?"

She pulls her hand out from under her head and holds up one finger.

"Then, fuck no. I don't want to know."

She chuckles. "Are you jealous at the thought of me being with two guys?"

"Babe, I'm jealous at the thought of you being with any other guys. Jesus. Was this at Northwestern? 'Cause I was kind of under the impression that you were..."

"What?" Her eyes narrow a little.

Word this very carefully, Cross. You're treading on thin ice here.

"You just didn't party much. And I don't remember you having a boyfriend at college."

"I didn't. And it wasn't at Northwestern."

"Thank God because there might have been a chance I knew the fuckers, and then I'd have to go kick the shit out of them."

She smiles and presses her hand to my cheek. "You're adorable."

"I'm not adorable. I'm a total badass. We've had this talk already. Do I need to remind you?"

"Nope." She presses her lips together, but her shoulders shake with laughter.

"You're not good for my ego, you know."

"Wild, you don't need my help with your ego. It's already bigger than the Grand Canyon."

Okay, so maybe I'm a little overly confident. But I have reason to be. I'm fucking awesome.

And I like that she just called me Wild.

"Say that again," I tell her.

"What?"

"Wild. You just called me it, and I want to hear you say it again."

She tips her head back a touch, and feline-like eyes stare at me. "Is this for ego purposes?"

"No." I push my hand under my head, resting on it, and stare back at her. "I just like hearing you say it."

She wets her lips with her tongue, and my dick twitches. Then, she moves closer, pressing her hand to my cheek, her thumb dusting over my lips, her own a breath away.

"Kiss me, Wild," she whispers.

So, I do. I wrap my arms around her and kiss her deeply, passionately…wildly.

When we finally break away, we're both breathless.

She rests her head against my chest. I slide my fingers into her hair, massaging the back of her head.

She lets out a sound of contentment, so I keep on massaging.

"How many girlfriends have you had?" she asks against my chest.

I stop massaging. "Are we back to this? Because, honestly, babe, I have zero desire to know how many guys you've dated."

"Three," she says. "And we were never on it. I just wondered."

Three? Did she not just hear what I said?

Fucking great. Now, I'm wondering who the hell these three guys were.

But I'm not asking. Because I'm not a masochist. Unlike a little someone who is currently plastered to my chest.

I let out a sigh and say, "None."

Her head comes up. "None?"

"Nope."

"How? I mean, I know you played the field in college—a lot of field—but I guess I just assumed you had at least one girlfriend after college."

"I've never been interested in tying myself down to just one woman." *Until now. Until you.*

"So, you've just spent the last nine years...like you did in college."

"Pretty much. You're actually the first woman I've had in my apartment—aside from my mom, that is. But she doesn't count."

"Thank God."

She laughs, and the sound is so fucking contagious, it has me laughing, too.

"I can't believe you've never brought anyone back here before." She pauses and bites her lip. "So...why did you bring me here then?"

Crappers. She's onto me.

"Because I wanted to." I shrug.

"Expand," she says.

And I know I'm not getting out of it.

I blow out a breath. "Because I wanted you here. Better?"

"A little. Why have you not brought anyone else to your apartment before?"

"Because I've never liked anyone enough to want them here."

Her eyes soften. "You like me?"

"Stop fishing for compliments. You know I like you. I've just spent the last few days with either my cock, tongue, or fingers inside you, so I'd say, it's pretty damn obvious by now that I like you."

She's smiling. "Well, it's a good thing I like you as well."

"You like me?" I point to my chest. "Or him?" I point down to my cock.

Even though I'm, like, ninety-five percent sure it's me she likes, I still need to hear her say it, and this was the perfect opportunity to ask.

"You're fishing," she teases.

"Absolutely, I am."

She smiles and presses her hand to my chest. "I like you. And him." She dips her chin south.

I chuckle. "Glad to hear it." I pull her close. "Because you sure as hell didn't like me in college."

She stiffens in my arms, and I figure this is the time to ask another question that's been bugging me.

"Why was that?"

"Why was what?" she asks against my chest.

I loosen my hold on her and tip her chin up with my hand, bringing her eyes to mine.

They're shuttered, and I don't like it. But it doesn't stop me from asking again.

"Why didn't you like me in college?"

She sighs and opens her eyes. "Do we really need to go over the past?"

"No. But I would like to know."

"Look...I guess...I just thought you were a bit of a man-whore. And I *incorrectly* thought that everything came easily to you. That you didn't have to work for anything. I know different now."

"I wish you'd known then."

Her brows pull together. "Why?"

"Because then maybe we'd have been doing this for the last thirteen years."

I brush my lips over hers, but she's unresponsive. Another thing I don't like.

"What's wrong?"

She bites the inside of her cheek. "Just...don't say things you don't mean."

It's my turn to frown. "Who says I don't mean it?"

"Me. Your endless stream of women in college."

"Just because I slept with a lot of women in college doesn't mean I would've done it if you and I had gotten together. I'm just saying that maybe things would've been different if you'd given me a chance."

I see something flash through her eyes, but it's gone before I can get ahold of it.

"Morgan?"

"What?"

"Is this our first fight?"

She lifts her eyes to mine. I see they've softened back to how I like them. Just like melted chocolate.

"I'm not fighting with you, Wilder."

"Good." I kiss the tip of her nose. "'Cause I'm not fighting with you either. Fucking? I'm all up for that. But not fighting."

I pull her head into my chest and kiss her hair.

She yawns, her hot breath brushing over my skin.

"Tired?" I ask her.

"Mmhmm. A little."

"You want to get in bed?"

"Soon," she murmurs.

But we never do make it to my bed, as we fall asleep right here, on the sofa, in each other's arms.

32

I wake up to the sound of my cell ringing.

We're still on the sofa. Morgan is plastered to my chest, like an electric blanket, but surprisingly, I like it.

I like having her here, sleeping with me.

It's something I was sure I would never want—until she came along, that is.

She stirs, groaning softly, as she comes around.

"Was that your phone?" she murmurs.

"Mmhmm."

"What time is it?"

"No clue." I rub the sleep from my eyes.

She pushes up from me and sits up, straddling my waist. The sheet that was covering us pools around her hips. Her hair is all mussed up from sleep. Her eyes lazily stare down at me.

She looks like a goddess.

My dick perks up and says, *Hello, baby.*

I've already got morning wood, but I'd be hard as a rock without it because that's the effect she has on me.

And it has been far too long since I was last inside her.

I slide my hands around her waist and lift her back to sit on my cock. She's hot and wet against my length. I bite back a moan.

Her eyes glitter with lust. She shifts her hips a touch, causing friction against my dick, and I see stars.

"Fuck," I groan. "Do that again."

"I will," she says. "But, first, I really need to use the bathroom."

"Aw, babe. You're killing me here. Can't you wait until we're done?" I rotate my hips, grinding against her pretty pussy, hoping to entice her to stay.

"Nope. Not unless you're into golden showers, that is."

She quirks a brow, and it's impossible not to laugh.

God, she's so frigging awesome.

"Go." I give her ass a pat. "And be quick."

She hops off me, and I watch her walk out of the room. I sit up and get my cell from the coffee table.

Jesus, it's two in the afternoon. And the missed call is from my mom.

I was supposed to check in with her and Dad when I got back last night, but I forgot because I had other things on my mind—Morgan—and also on my cock—also Morgan.

I hit redial and put the phone to my ear.

"He's alive!" my mom calls out in a teasing voice.

"Sorry, I meant to call."

"Well, as long as you're okay. I was just about to send your father round to your place to check on you."

Good thing I called then; otherwise, my dad would have gotten one hell of an eyeful of his other CEO.

"I'm fine."

"How was Thailand?"

"Great."

"And Ananda?"

"Good."

"Have I gone back in time about twenty years?"

"What?"

"You and the one-worded answers. It's like having a conversation with preteen Wilder."

"Funny." I roll my eyes, like a preteen. "Sorry, I'm just tired." I rub my eyes again.

"Are you jet-lagged?"

"Yeah." *And worn out from all the sex I've been having with Morgan.* But we'll leave that little nugget of info out of the conversation.

"Okay, darling. We'll talk properly when we're back in the office, but I just wanted to check that everything went well with Ananda."

"Yeah, it went fine. Niran's great, really easy to get along with, which will help when dealing with him going forward. The factory setup is perfect. They have definite room for expansion, too, if needed. And the material…it's top-notch. You're gonna be really happy with it."

"And Morgan? How did she get on?"

Well, Mom, she got on and off quite a lot of times over the last few days.

But I'm pretty sure that's not what you meant.

"She did great. Really great. Did you know that she speaks four foreign languages?"

My mom chuckles. "Of course I knew. I saw her résumé when we approached her to hire her."

Duh. Course she did.

"Yeah, well, it was cool that she was able to converse with Niran and his wife in their own language. I think it really made a difference, you know."

"Yeah. Anyway, I won't keep you, honey. Go get some sleep, and I'll talk to you on Monday."

"Okay, Mom."

I hang up and place my cell on the table.

"So, I did great, huh?"

I turn my head to the sound of Morgan's voice.

She's standing in the doorway that leads to the hallway, leaning against the frame. And she's no longer naked. She's wearing the T-shirt I gave her last night.

"You're dressed." I frown. "Didn't we have a whole conversation about not wearing clothes?"

Her eyebrow lifts, and I know she's waiting for an answer to her question.

"Yes, you did great work with Ananda, but you already knew that. Now, take the fucking T-shirt off," I command.

She pushes off the doorframe and yanks the T-shirt over her head, dropping it to the floor.

"Better?" she says with sass.

God, she's fucking sexy. I am the luckiest bastard ever.

"Much." I swing my legs up onto the sofa and recline back. I take my cock in my hand and give him a firm upstroke.

Her eyes ignite like a match has just been struck behind them. "So, where were we before I went to the bathroom?" Her voice sounds husky with sex.

I tip my cock in her direction. "You were about to climb up on here and give me the ride of my life."

She lifts her hand, revealing a condom in it. "Well then, we'd better saddle you up, cowboy."

She rips open the condom with her teeth and saunters over to me with a hot promise in her eyes. And I can't fucking wait to take her up on it.

33

Morgan is lying on top of me, still catching her breath. And just here, under her, I'm basking in the afterglow of my latest orgasm, tracing lazy patterns on her back.

I don't think I've ever been this happy. I feel euphoric. Like I'm hopped up on drugs.

I remember this time when I was at Columbia, and Coop and Dom came to visit. Coop hooked up with this chick who turned out to be big into her drugs. Anyway, she took us to this party, and she gave us each an ecstasy pill—which, of course, was a very wrong thing to do.

Don't do drugs, kids! Stay in school!

Anyway, I'd never done ecstasy before. I'd smoked weed and snorted coke a couple of times, but I'd never popped pills. But I thought, *Fuck it*, so I swallowed it down. At first, nothing happened, and then, all of a sudden, it was like everything changed. Everything became clearer and brighter. Like the whole world was in Technicolor.

I loved everything and everyone. I'm pretty sure I even told a homeless guy that I loved him and that he should come stay with me in my dorm after we left the club.

Basically, I was as high as a kite.

But, for that brief time, I felt fucking awesome.

And that's how I feel right now, here with Morgan. Only this time, I don't need to take drugs to reach that high.

All I need is *her*.

I know some of the way I'm feeling right now probably has to do with all the oxytocin and endorphins constantly flooding my system at the moment. But I also know that it is because of Morgan.

She's perfect.

Honestly, everything she does is awesome.

She could fart, and I swear, I'd smell roses.

And you know what? I'm not even scared of the effect she's having on me.

It's in fact the total opposite.

I frigging love the effect she has on me.

Seriously, who knew another person could make you feel this way? Like I'm a king who's permanently high on ecstasy.

I can't believe what I've been missing out on all these years.

"You okay under there?" Morgan mumbles against my chest. "I'm not squashing you, am I?"

Laughter rumbles in my chest. "You weigh about a buck twenty, babe. I bench-press twice that at the gym. So, no, you're not squashing me."

She peels herself off my chest and sits up.

I can see her eyes carefully assessing me as she starts to chew on the inside of her cheek. "Wilder, I weigh one thirty-five on a good day. Is that gonna be a problem?"

My brows shove together in confusion. "No. But I'm interested to know why you think it would be."

She shrugs, her eyes moving from me to stare out the window.

I sit up and take her chin in my hand. I tug her face back around to mine.

"What's going on, babe?"

"Nothing."

She says nothing, but there's clearly something. Aside from the fact that she's practically gnawing off the inside of her cheek, she can barely look at me.

Does she have body issues?

I wouldn't have thought so. She hasn't tried to hide herself from me. But I definitely know something is bothering her.

"Babe, I think you're fucking gorgeous. Your body is off the charts." I let my eyes roam down her, taking her in, and my dick starts to harden in response. I grab her hand and put it against my cock. "You feel that? I came about ten minutes ago, and I'm hard as stone already. That is all *you*."

Her eyes dip to my cock. Then, she lifts them back to me.

She exhales a slow breath, and then she leans in and kisses me.

I sink my hand into her hair, fisting it as I deepen the kiss, taking control.

I drag my mouth down her neck. "I can't get enough of you," I say against her soft skin. "It's never been this way for me before."

"Me either," she whispers.

I lift my mouth back to hers, and our lips crash together.

This kiss isn't about sex even though I could definitely go again.

It's about something more. Something deeper.

She kisses the corner of my mouth, my cheek, my eyelid, my forehead, peppering me with kisses.

Then, her stomach rumbles loudly, breaking the moment.

"Shit, sorry." She laughs, pressing her hand to it.

"You hungry?" I chuckle.

"I guess I am."

"Let's feed you then. What are you in the mood for? We'll order in."

She cocks a brow at me. "Don't you ever cook?"

"Not unless I have to."

"And when have you ever had to?"

I think this over, tapping my finger to my lips. "Um…the 2011 blizzard. No one was delivering."

She rolls her eyes at me. "Come on, let's cook something. It'll be fun." She climbs off me and goes to retrieve my T-shirt off the floor before pulling it on.

I frown. "I can think of more fun things to do."

Her hands go to her hips. "Such as?"

"Order in."

"Stop being a lazy ass. Come on," she coaxes.

Sighing, I get to my feet. Guess I'm gonna need clothes as well if she's making me cook. I look around for my pajama pants, but I can't see them.

"I'm just gonna grab some pants. I'll meet you in the kitchen." I slap her ass as I pass her, making her squeal.

Smiling all the way to my bedroom, I grab some clean pants and then dip into the bathroom to give my teeth a quick brush.

When I get to the kitchen, she's sitting on the counter with a glass of water, waiting for me.

I go over to her, positioning myself between her legs. I take the glass from her and have a drink before handing it back to her.

"So, what are we making?" I ask her.

She puts the glass down. "How do you feel about waffles?"

"It's the food of gods."

Under HER

She smiles. "Well, I was thinking I could make us banana waffles with Nutella if you have any. I make the best banana waffles known to man."

"Marry me," I say.

She laughs.

But I'm only half-kidding.

She makes waffles and fucks like a porn star.

She's frigging perfect.

She presses a kiss to the tip of my nose. Then, she hops down off the counter, and we get to work.

Morgan's just mixing up the waffle batter when my phone chimes a text.

It's Coop in our group chat.

> Coop: What's the plan for tonight? We doing the usual?

Shit. It's Saturday. Boys' night. I didn't even think about it.

"Everything all right?" Morgan asks.

I realize I've been staring at my phone for a while.

"Yeah, fine. It's just Coop."

I look back at my phone and tap out a reply.

> Me: I can't make it tonight. Sorry, guys. Next week for sure.

He replies a few seconds later.

> Coop: You'd better be either dying or getting your cock serviced by a porn star if you're ducking out on tonight.

I chuckle to myself and glance over at Morgan, who's pouring the batter onto the waffle maker.

Me: No, to the first. And, yes, to the second but not by a porn star.

By someone way, way better than a porn star.

Coop: You're off the hook. You can tell me all the deets at brunch tomorrow.

I hesitate. I don't want to flake out on my boys twice in a row. But I've got Morgan here. If I go to brunch, she'll leave, and I don't know when she'll come back.

"You're awfully quiet over there. Are you just pretending to text to get out of cooking?"

I lift my eyes to her smiling ones.

"Me? Never. No, I'm just texting Coop about tomorrow."

"What's tomorrow?"

"I, um…I always have brunch with him and Dom on Sunday."

"Okay. Cool. I can head off first thing."

"Or you can come with me."

Her eyes flash with surprise. Honestly, I surprised myself by saying it. But I don't want to take it back either. I want her to come with me.

"I don't want to intrude."

Putting my phone down, I walk over to her. The smell of waffles fills my nose.

"You wouldn't be intruding. You know Coop and Dom. And it'd be good for you all to catch up. It's been a while."

She's staring up at me, chewing on the inside of her cheek, indecision in her eyes. "Okay. But only if it's okay with them."

I kiss her forehead. "It will be."

Under Her

I retrieve my phone from the counter. There's a message from Dom now that makes me laugh.

> **Dom:** I'm still on for tonight. Unlike Cross, who's ditching us for pussy.
>
> **Me:** Jealous much? And it's funny how you've forgotten that time when you ditched us two weeks in a row because you were too busy banging that dental hygienist from Springfield.
>
> **Coop:** He's got you there, Dom.

Dom replies with the middle finger emoji. I snigger and then tap out a reply.

> **Me:** I'll see you both at brunch tomorrow. And I'm bringing a friend.
>
> **Coop:** Is it the current cock servicer by any chance?
>
> **Me:** Maybe.
>
> **Coop:** And does this cock servicer go by the name of Morgan by any chance?

My eyes scan the kitchen, like I expect Coop to jump out at any second.

> **Me:** Maybe.

Coop: Ha! I fucking knew it. Dom, you owe me ten Gs.

Me: Um, what?

Dom: Ah, for fuck's sake. You could've kept it zipped, Wilder. You just cost me ten grand.

Me: Does anyone want to tell me what the fuck is going on?

Coop: I bet Dom ten Gs that you'd nail Morgan in Thailand. He said you wouldn't. Thus, he loses.

Me: Who said I nailed Morgan in Thailand?

Dom: You saying you didn't, Wild? Because I've got ten grand riding on this.

Me: I seriously can't believe you assholes bet ten Gs on Morgan and me hooking up. You're a pair of pricks.

Coop: You're surprised? This is me and Dom you're talking about.

Me: True.

Dom: So…

Me: You owe the man ten grand.

> Dom: For fuck's sake. I'll pay you tonight, Coop.
>
> Coop: ☺ See you tomorrow, Wild. And tell Morgan I said hi. Oh, wait, don't bother. I'll just tell her myself at brunch tomorrow.

I reply with the middle finger emoji and shut off my phone.

The smell of waffles wafts under my nose, and I glance up to see Morgan walking toward me, two plates of waffles in her hands.

I give her a guilty look. "Shit. Sorry, babe. I didn't exactly help."

"It's okay." She hands me my plate and heads for the kitchen door. "You can just pay me back later in orgasms."

See? Didn't I tell you she was frigging perfect?

My gorgeous waffle girl.

34

Morgan is fidgeting beside me as we walk into Sonny's, the best waffle and pancake house in Chicago, to meet Coop and Dom.

I know she's nervous. But I have no clue why.

She already knows them both, and she used to work with Dom at Starbucks.

If anyone should be worried, it's me. I know they're both gonna give me shit for bringing a girl to brunch, meaning they'll pull out all the old stories to make me look like a prick in front of Morgan. And that's not them being jerks. It's just a guy thing. I'd do exactly the same thing to them if one of them turned up with a chick in tow.

I squeeze Morgan's hand that I'm holding, and she looks up at me.

"Relax, babe. It's just brunch with the boys."

She blows out a breath. "I know. You're right. I don't know why I'm so nervous."

"Because you're adorable." I smile at her before bringing my mouth down to her ear. "Look, we'll stay an hour, max, and then we'll go back to my apartment. Where I'll strip off your clothes and put you in my shower. I want to try out the massage setting on you. I'm interested to see how long it'll take you to come if I use it on your pussy."

I chuckle darkly at the sharp breath she inhales. I press a soft kiss to her neck before moving away. But I daren't meet her eyes because I know what will be in them, and I know that it'll have me hard in seconds.

I lead us over to our usual table. Coop and Dom are already here. Coop grins at me. Then, his eyes land on Morgan, and they widen a touch. I know that look on him, and I know exactly what he's thinking.

I feel a surge of possessiveness over Morgan. Something I've never felt around a woman before. Previously, I would never have cared if Coop had thought a chick I was nailing was hot. Hell, I would've stepped aside for him if he'd asked me.

But not for Morgan.

She's mine.

"Assholes," I greet them with a cocky grin. "You remember Morgan."

"Sure I do." Dom gets to his feet and leans over to kiss her cheek.

And I want to punch him.

Jesus, I've got it bad.

"You look great, Morgan," Dom says to her.

"Yeah, you really do." Coop stands and kisses her cheek. As he pulls back, the fucker meets my eyes and grins.

He definitely thinks she's hot, and he's going to flirt like fuck with her.

Not because he's an asshole—well, he is an asshole—but this is his way of winding me up. Payback for missing out on boys' night.

Us guys are total jerks at times.

Under
HER

But I can't say I wouldn't do the same to him 'cause I totally would.

"You've gone from pretty college chick to hot-as-fuck businesswoman."

Jesus, Coop. You're laying it on a bit thick.

"What the hell are you doing with this asshole?" He thumbs in my direction.

I resist flipping him off. Then, I notice that Morgan's blushing. And *that*, I definitely don't like.

Possessiveness swoops in again like a bitch, and I sling my arm over her shoulders, pulling her closer to me.

Coop smirks, and I narrow my eyes on him.

"You're right; she is too good for me. But, luckily for me, she sees something in me and wants to be with me anyway."

Shit, did that sound a bit pussified?

But, the instant Morgan glances up at me, my worry disappears. The softness in her eyes does something weird to my chest.

"I don't just see something in you, Cross. I see a lot in you." She smiles at me, and that weird feeling in my chest intensifies.

"Jesus. Knock it off with the lovefest, will ya? Or I'm gonna hurl, and I haven't even had my food yet."

This time, I do flip Coop off.

I pull out a chair for Morgan and then take the one beside her.

I rest my arm over the back of it and stroke the bare skin on her arm with my fingers because I have to touch her.

"You guys order yet?" I ask them.

"Nah, we were waiting for you," Dom answers.

"What do you want, babe?" I ask Morgan. I already know what I'm having.

She picks up the menu and quickly glances over it.

"I'll have the Healthy Waffles and a coffee."

"Is there such a thing as Healthy Waffles?" Dom chuckles.

"Probably not." Morgan laughs. "But it definitely makes me feel better about having waffles twice in two days."

"Get used to it," Coops says to her. "One-third of Wild's diet is waffles."

"And what are the other two-thirds?" she asks him, smiling.

"Coffee and sex, of course." He grins, and she blushes.

But he's not wrong.

Our waitress comes over, and we all order. I, of course, order my usual—Chicago's Best, which is basically waffles with everything.

The waitress has just brought our coffees over when Coop leans forward, elbows on the table, and puts all his focus on Morgan. "So, Morgan, tell us about what you've been up to since college."

She chuckles. "That's a whole lot of years' worth of stuff to tell you."

"I've got the time. In fact, I have all the time in the world for you."

I scowl at him. "That's because you're a lazy fuck who doesn't work like the rest of us."

Coop grins at me and sits back in his chair. "True. But maybe I should work because, if all women in business look like Morgan, then work is definitely a place I want to be."

"They don't all look like Morgan. Believe me," Dom imparts, chuckling. "You've met Sonja, my relationship specialist," he says to Coop, whose face screws up at the mention of her.

"Ugh, fuck yeah." Coop shudders. "That chick has warts on warts. How the fuck is she a specialist on relationships? I bet the only relationship she's ever had is with Pornhub and her vibrator."

Under HER

"Jesus, dude." I throw a rolled up napkin at him. "Woman at the table." *My* woman, to be exact.

"Don't worry about me," Morgan says. "I've heard worse."

I want to ask from where, but then she looks at Coop and says, "And don't knock the education that Pornhub and a vibrator can give a girl. I can tell you from experience that I've learned some of my best relationship moves from Pornhub and BOB." She winks, and my mouth drops open.

Coop hoots out a laugh. Dom nearly chokes on his coffee.

I'm staring at Morgan like I'm seeing her for the first time.

I know she's open in bed, and I also, unfortunately, know that she's had a threesome with two other dudes. But she's only open when she's turned on. When she's not and the subject of sex comes up, she goes shy. So, to hear her say something so fucking open and sexual and, quite frankly, hot as fuck in front of Coop and Dom, it shocks the hell out of me. And it also makes me a lot hard.

I'm quickly working out if I can get away with dragging her to the restroom for a quickie when Coop bangs his hand on the table, still laughing.

"Fucking hell, Wild!" He chortles. "You've got your hands full with this one."

I stare over at her. Her eyes are glittering with humor, and I smile big.

"I know," I say. Then, I wrap my arm around her neck and pull her close to me, planting a kiss on her forehead.

And I don't mind one fucking bit. Because I want all of me to be full of her. My hands. My head. And my heart.

35

Morgan and I are lying in my bed on our sides, facing each other. And, of course, we're both naked.

Morgan's fingers are sifting through my hair, and I'm beyond relaxed.

After we got back from brunch, we took a shower together, and I tried out the massage setting on her, like I'd said I would.

Let's just say, it works really well. She came like a motherfucker. And the blow job I received afterward in thanks had my eyes rolling back in my head.

"Brunch was fun," she says softly. "It was nice, seeing Dom and Cooper again."

"Yeah. They enjoyed seeing you, too." And I know that for a fact because they both texted me afterward to tell me in their own unique ways that they thought Morgan was awesome and that I should bring her to brunch more often.

And I want to.

I want to bring her with me every fucking week. I want to be with her at work all day and have her in my bed every night.

But I still don't know where she's at on the subject of us. If she even sees me and her as an us.

All I know is that I'm fucking crazy about her, and I want her in every way possible. I'm hoping that she wants the same.

"I can't believe it's Sunday already." She sighs. "The weekend has gone by so fast but slow as well, if you know what I mean."

"Yeah." I know exactly what she means.

"Back to work tomorrow," she says. The way she says it doesn't sound entirely happy, and I take that as a positive sign.

I know she loves her job, so I'm hoping it's because she doesn't want this right here between us to end.

She starts to massage my scalp with her fingers, and it feels frigging amazing. My eyes close at the sensation.

"Wilder…"

"Morgan."

"Can I talk to you about something?"

I pop one eye open. Then, the other joins it.

"Sure." My heart starts to beat a little faster in my chest.

"Well…" She pauses and chews on the corner of her lip. "I was just wondering…"

"What?" *Say it, for Christ's sake, because I'm fucking dying here.*

"What is…this?" She points her finger to my chest and then hers.

I hold back the smile I feel. Because she's just shown me her hand. She's so on the fucking same page as me that we could write a book together.

But, now that I know she wants an us, I decide to play with her a little.

I might be crazy about her, but this is me we're talking about here.

"What is what?" I glance down at my chest, then to hers, and then back to her face.

Her brows are furrowed. "This...us...what we're doing here."

"Well, babe, it's called fucking. But I thought you knew that already."

"Funny. Asshole." She shoves away from me, rolling onto her back.

I follow her, chuckling. I roll on top of her, taking her in my arms. I stare down at her. "I'm messing with you, babe."

I brush my lips over hers and meet resistance at first, but she caves quickly.

"What do you want this to be?"

"I asked first."

"Well"—I kiss her again—"I was kinda hoping that we'd keep doing what we're doing."

She lets out a breath, her eyes going to the ceiling.

Okay, so that's not the response I was hoping for.

Shit. Maybe I read this wrong, and she doesn't want a relationship.

"Look, Wilder..."

Her eyes come back to mine, but I can't read them.

Jesus...is she about to give me the it-was-fun-an'-all-but-I'm-done line?

"I know how you live your life, and I think I might have given you the wrong impression when I told you that I had a threesome. But I was actually in a relationship with one of the guys when that happened. It was something that my boyfriend at the time wanted to try. He was bisexual. And I wasn't really sure, but I did it for him. Anyway...it actually ended up breaking us up because it made me all paranoid that I wasn't enough for him.

"So, what I'm trying to say is that I'm not the kind of girl who can share. And, if I'm with someone, then I'm with *only* him. One-night stands or weekend hook-ups aren't usually my thing, but this is you, and…" She blows out a breath. "Look, I understand if you want to leave it here. I just wanted you to know that I can't be with you while you're with other women."

Can I just say that my heart is doing cartwheels in my chest right now? In a totally manly way, of course.

"Babe"—I frame her face with my hands—"I don't know if you've noticed, but I'm not exactly interested in anyone else right now."

"But what if—"

"There are no what-ifs. I'm mad about you, Morgan. And I have been since the day I walked into my office and saw you sitting there. I don't and I won't ever want anyone else but you."

She smiles, and it's fucking incandescent. "Really?"

"Really." I smile.

"And what about work?" she asks.

"What about work?"

"Well, how is this…us being together, going to work there?"

I shrug. "I figure it'll be the same as before—except, now, I get to nail you on my desk anytime I want."

She laughs, shaking her head. "I meant, with everyone else."

"Well, I wasn't planning on inviting them to watch, babe."

"I mean, do you think we should keep our relationship under wraps for the time being?"

"Huh. I don't know. Maybe. Is that what you want?"

"I don't want to hide us, but then I also think maybe we should."

"Because of our seniority at the company?"

"Yeah, that, and…"

"You're worried about my mom and dad."

She bites the inside of her cheek. "Yeah...but I also feel a bit weird about Sierra."

"Sierra? Why?" I frown.

Her eyes lock on to mine. "Because you slept with her."

"So?" I shrug, and instantly, I realize it was the wrong thing to do. "Babe, there's nothing to feel weird about. What Sierra and I had...well, we didn't have anything. It was a one-off. It meant nothing."

"To you maybe. But she did try to seduce you that time in your office, and I see the way she looks at you."

"She doesn't look at me in any way."

Morgan rolls her eyes at me, like I'm clueless. "I'm her boss, Wilder, and I don't like knowing that she knows you like I know you."

"She doesn't know me like you do." *No one does.*

"I meant, in the biblical sense. She's seen you naked."

"Oh, well, if it helps, I don't know what she looks like biblically. To be honest, I don't really remember anything about that night."

"It doesn't help. Not one little bit."

"Okay, so I should just keep my mouth shut about it then."

"Probably best."

Eyes on the ceiling, her mouth knitted into a tight line, she starts chewing on the inside of her cheek again.

"Babe..."

"Mmhmm?"

"I'm sorry."

She brings her eyes back to mine.

"For the Sierra thing," I clarify.

"It's not your fault." She sighs. "You couldn't have known that I was going to hire her. And it's my issue to get past."

"Well, even so, I am sorry."

She brushes her fingers over my cheek. "I'm sorry it bothers me so much."

"Babe, trust me, if this were the other way around, I'd have beaten the guy to death by now."

She giggles, but I'm not fucking kidding. Just the thought of her and another guy makes me want to commit murder.

"Wilder?"

"Mmhmm?"

"Kiss me."

I lower my mouth to hers and kiss her soft, unhurried.

But that doesn't last long; it never does with us.

Soon, we're writhing and clawing at each other's bodies, and I'm desperate to be inside her.

I reach for the drawer on my nightstand where I put the condoms.

I'd never kept them in there before, always in my wallet or my car. I'd never had a reason to keep them in my nightstand because I never fucked anyone in here—until her.

I locate the box and—

Fuck, it's empty.

"Shit." I groan, dropping my head to her shoulder.

She's panting beneath me. "What?"

"I'm out of rubbers."

"Shit," she breathes. "What are we gonna do?"

"Well, I can either run to the store with a stiffy. Or we go oral. Your call, babe. But so you know, I can't run fast with a boner."

She giggles, but it fades off quickly. "There is a third option," she says quietly.

I know exactly what she's thinking because, honestly, the thought has crossed my mind, too. And not just now, but at other times as well.

I've never gone without a condom before. Aside from STDs, can anyone say *unwanted pregnancy*?

Under
HER

But the thought of being with her, like that, it does something to me that I can't explain.

"Is that something…you would want?"

She blinks up at me, eyes wide. "Yeah. I mean, I'm on the pill. I'm clean. And I trust you, Wilder."

The knowledge of that, that she trusts me, tears my chest wide open. "I trust you, too, babe. And I'm clean. I swear."

She lifts up, bringing her mouth close to mine, and she stares into my eyes. "I trust you," she reiterates. Then, she kisses me.

I grab a handful of her hair and angle her head, taking over the kiss. I kiss her hard, thrusting my tongue into her mouth.

Kneeing her legs apart, I settle her head back down to the pillow and come to rest between her legs.

I can feel her damp heat pressing against my cock.

Keeping my mouth on hers, I lift my hips, rubbing my length along her pussy. Then, finding her entrance, I push the tip of my cock inside. "Fuck. Oh, fuck. Oh, fuck."

She's hot and snug and…like nothing I've ever felt.

I keep pushing inside her until I'm in to the hilt.

I hold still, my dick throbbing inside her. Her pussy feels like a tight, wet fist around my cock.

"Wilder…please…I need you to move," she whimpers.

"Just…" My eyes are squeezed shut. Sweat is beading on my forehead. "Babe, if I move, I'll come."

"I don't care." She kisses me. "I need you."

She needs me.

My eyes flash open. I pull out to the tip and slam back inside.

"Yes! Like that! Keep doing that. Fuck me, Wilder."

My control snaps, and I start thrusting my cock in and out of her. Harder with every move.

"You. Feel. Fucking. Incredible," I grind out. My hips are snapping back and forth, my balls slapping her ass. I tilt forward a touch, knowing that the angle will cause my cock to rub against her clit.

"God, Wilder. If you keep doing that, you're gonna make me come."

"That's the plan, baby." I grin cockily. Then, I make the mistake of meeting her eyes, and all my bravado slips away.

Have you ever been to the top of a really tall building?

I have. About five years ago, I was in Shanghai on business, and while I was there, I went to the Oriental Pearl Tower. It has a glass sightseeing floor about a thousand feet up from the ground.

It's the weirdest sensation, being up there, standing on it. Knowing that the only thing keeping you from falling is a glass floor.

It's like fear and exhilaration, all at the same time.

And that's what I feel like right now, staring down into Morgan's eyes.

"Wilder," she moans.

Her body contracts as she starts to come, which triggers my own orgasm. Bare for the first time ever, I come, spilling everything I have inside her.

"Wow," she whispers. "That was…wow."

"Yeah." But I can barely speak because it's all so suddenly clear. The inability to want anyone but her. The need to be with her all the fucking time.

"Hey, you okay?" She runs her fingers over my cheek.

"What? Oh, yeah, I'm fine."

"You sure? Because you look…"

She tilts her head to the side, appraising me, and I swear, I stop breathing because I'm sure she can see it written all over my face.

"I don't know. You look different somehow."

I swallow down. "It's probably just because we had sex without a condom for the first time."

"Yeah? And how was that for you?"

Well…

"It was good," I croak out.

She laughs. "Don't go crazy there, Wilder."

Yeah, because the last thing we want is for me to go crazy and realize something, like...oh, I don't know...that I'm madly in love with you.

Oops. Already did that.

Fuck.

36

I've had the best few weeks of my life.

I wake up beside Morgan. We have breakfast together and then come to work. We have sex in my office. We don't fuck in Morgan's because she still feels weird about the Sierra thing, and she doesn't want Sierra to find out about us. Chrissy knows. But she can be trusted.

Then, after work, we go home together to either my place or hers. Eat dinner. Sometimes, we watch *Breaking Bad*. Mostly, we have sex. Then, we fall asleep together. And do it all over again the next day.

And it's awesome.

I didn't know it was possible to spend this much time with someone and not get bored. Let alone feel like it's not enough.

It's like nothing will ever be enough with her. I'll always want more.

She's become the center of my universe. If you think about it, it should be pretty fucking scary that I feel so strongly about her in such a short space of time, but I can't find it in me to care.

Because being in love with Morgan is the best feeling in the whole fucking world.

And, okay, maybe I haven't told her *exactly* how I feel about her.

As in she doesn't know that I'm in love with her.

I'm working up to it. I just need to find the right moment. Telling someone that you love them isn't something you can blurt out.

Especially when I don't know if she feels the same.

I mean, I'm almost sure that she feels the same as I do. I think I see it in her eyes when she looks at me and feel it in her body when we make love.

But it hasn't been confirmed to me.

And, yeppers, I've reached the make-love stage. Of course, I still fuck her because I'm me. But I make love to her, too. And it's amazing.

Life is amazing.

We've been making plans. Nothing major, just things we want to do together. And I'm meeting her friends this weekend. We're going out to dinner with her best friend, Joely, and her husband, Todd.

I do remember Joely, but I didn't really know her that well back in college. Apparently, her husband went to Northwestern as well. Morgan told me that was where they met. At a college party, I think she said.

I'm just looking forward to meeting the important people in her life. Last night, she even mentioned us going to visit her parents for a weekend.

Sounds like a big step, right? But, honestly, it doesn't feel like it. And it's not like she hasn't met my parents.

Everything with Morgan feels natural and right. I'm disgustingly and nauseatingly in love with her.

Thy name is Wilder, and I am pussy-whipped.

And I've never been happier.

Under HER

But it's always the times when you're at your happiest that things go to shit.

Because, when things go up, they always have to come down.

My desk phone rings, and I pick it up.

"Wilder, it's Mom."

"Hey, how are you doing? How's the cruise?"

Surprisingly, to me and everyone else here—because, even though they retired, they were still here all the goddamn time—my mom and dad booked a last-minute cruise to the Caribbean. They set sail a week ago.

I've been getting regular text updates from them, but this is the first phone call.

"Fine. Look, that's not what I'm calling about. Have you seen the business news today?"

"No. Why?"

"Because Coveted Lingerie just announced a new line. A plus-sized line."

"What? You mean…"

"Yes."

Shit.

Coveted Lingerie is our biggest competition.

I sit forward and bring up a search engine on my computer. I type in *Coveted Lingerie*, and sure enough, in the news section, there is their announcement of a luxury line of plus-sized bras at affordable costs.

"I just…how the hell?"

"That's what your dad and I want to know. I thought Morgan said that Ananda was the cheapest supplier around."

"She did. They are."

"Then, Coveted Lingerie would have to be making the bras at a loss, and I can't see that happening, Wilder."

No, she's right. They wouldn't.

"Maybe they found another supplier. One that Morgan didn't know about. Or they struck a deal with one of their current suppliers."

"Possibly. But, however they did it, they beat us to the punch."

"Fuck. We should have announced sooner."

I wanted to announce, but Morgan said we should wait until production was underway.

Morgan.

She's going to be devastated. This was her deal. Her idea.

"I need to call Morgan," I tell Mom. "Let her know what's happening."

"And call Niran while you're at it. See if he can push production forward. We might be able to salvage this if we can get our line out before Coveted releases theirs. It's not ideal, but it's all we've got left."

"You're right. I'll get on it straightaway. I'll call you back when I know more."

I hang up with Mom and dial straight through to Morgan's office.

Sierra answers, "Hi, Wilder. She's in a meeting with HR at the moment. I can get her to call you when she's done if you'd like."

"How long has she been in the meeting?"

"Oh, thirty minutes or so."

I could get her to interrupt, but something stops me. "Okay. Just get her to call me the second she's out."

"Will do."

I hang up and tap my fingers on the desk.

I really do need to talk to Morgan, but honestly, the thought of telling her makes me want to puke. I know how gutted she's going to be.

Totally different circumstance because this isn't Morgan's fault, but I remember when I screwed up the Renshaw deal. I felt like shit for ages afterward.

Maybe I could call Niran myself and see how things stand with moving production forward. I could get him to a workable date that would bring us ahead of Coveted's release. It wouldn't fix things, but at least it would cushion the blow for her.

It's morning here, so it's late in Thailand, but I need to speak with him. I pick up my phone and dial the cell number I have for Niran.

He answers on the fourth ring.

"Niran, it's Wilder Cross. I'm sorry to call so late."

"It's fine! No problem at all. It is good to hear from you. I wanted to speak to you, say how sorry I was to hear that your company no longer required your order—"

"I'm sorry, what?"

"Your order of silk. Morgan called me, oh, a few days ago to cancel. She said that you had found a cheaper supplier and would be purchasing from them. I was very disappointed to find that out because I thought we could do great business together, but I couldn't go any lower on the price."

"She canceled the order? Morgan did?"

"Yes. I have it in writing, too. She emailed it to me after we talked on the telephone."

I can't breathe. I'm having a heart attack. Or a panic attack. Or both.

Fuck.

"Wilder? Are you still there?"

"Yes, I'm still here. So, let me get this straight." I rub my fingers against the pressure building in my forehead. "You're telling me that Morgan—my Morgan, Morgan Stickford—called you up a few days ago and canceled our order of silk. And that she confirmed it in writing on the same day."

"Yes. Was she not supposed to do that?"

No, Niran. She fucking wasn't.

"No, she wasn't," I tell him. "So, we need to reinstate the order, Niran."

And then I'm going to strangle Morgan after I find out what the fuck she was thinking.

"Oh, I'm sorry, Wilder. I sold the silk to another company. They contacted me not long after Morgan canceled the order. A few hours maybe. It was luck really."

I swallow back the bile rising in my throat. "What's the name of the company you sold the silk to?"

"Coveted Lingerie."

37

I shove open Morgan's office door with so much force that it slams into the wall, shaking the room.

Morgan, Polly, and Chester all jump in their seats, like a shot was just fired.

"Oh my God!" Morgan gasps, pressing a hand to her chest. "You scared the crap out of me."

I scared her. Funny that.

Because, right now, I feel like killing her.

"Wilder?" Her brows draw together. "Is everything all right?"

"Chester, Polly, your meeting is over. Go back to your offices." I don't take my eyes off Morgan.

At first, they don't move. Then, Morgan gives them a nod. They both gather up their things and walk quickly out of her office, closing the door behind them.

"What's going on?" she asks, getting to her feet.

"I just got off the phone with Niran."

Her face drops. "Has something happened with the silk? Is that what's wrong?"

Seriously? This is the way she's going to play it? The innocent card?

"I don't know, Morgan. You would know more about that than I would. I mean, this is your deal after all."

"I haven't spoken to him recently. But, the last time I did, everything was on track. What did he say when you spoke to him?"

I want to laugh. Not the funny, ha-ha kind of laugh. The are-you-fucking-kidding-me laugh.

"So, the last time you spoke to him, everything was still on track?"

"That's what I just said. Seriously, Wilder, what's going on with you? You're acting kind of weird."

I do laugh this time. It sounds kind of maniacal. "Well, it's funny because that's not what Niran says your last phone call was about. According to him, you called him up a few days ago and canceled the order."

"What?" She steps back, her face blanching.

Oh, she's good.

From that reaction, I would almost believe that was the first time she was hearing it.

"Oh, yeah, and that's not all he said. He also told me that you confirmed it with him in email. And he was kind enough to send me a copy of it." I reach into my pocket and toss the folded-up paper version of the email that I just printed off.

"I don't understand." She picks the paper up, opens it, and reads it, her eyes scanning the paper. "This isn't...I didn't write this email."

"Like you didn't give your idea to Coveted Lingerie and then pull our order from Niran, so they could take over the deal instead."

"No!" she gasps. "That doesn't even make any sense! I don't even know anyone at Coveted Lingerie!"

"Sure you don't."

"I don't! This was my idea!" She slams a hand to her chest. "Why would I give it to them when I work here for you? Think logically, Wilder. It doesn't make sense."

"I have thought about it. Maybe Coveted offered you more money. A better position in the company. Who the fuck knows? But what I do know is, you canceled the silk order with Ananda two days ago. And then, a few hours later, Coveted contacted Niran and bought up all the silk from our canceled order. And, just under an hour ago, they announced their brand-new range of plus-sized luxury bras at affordable prices."

"No." Her hand covers her mouth.

I see her hand shaking, but I can't register anything but the blind rage I feel at her betrayal.

"But…but they can't do that. Niran can't do that! He can't just sell our silk to them. He signed a contract with us."

"Which you canceled."

"I didn't cancel it!"

"Just stop, Morgan. Just fucking stop. I've heard enough of the lies. I know the truth. And, now, I'm telling you that you're fired. Effective immediately. You've got ten minutes to pack your shit and get out."

Her lip trembles, eyes glazing with tears.

But I don't feel a damn thing. It's like my brain shut down all sense of feeling the second I realized that Morgan had betrayed me. Leaving me with the only source of emotion that I'm currently capable of feeling—anger.

I watch as she sucks in a breath. Then, she turns and walks away from me, going behind her desk. When she turns back around, her face is a mask.

"Fine," she says, her voice stiff and cold. "But expect a call from my lawyer first thing tomorrow morning for unfair dismissal."

Well, if those words aren't like gasoline to my already-roaring flame.

I let out a disgusted laugh.

I can't believe I loved this woman.

Still do love this woman.

"You're fucking unbelievable." I take large, menacing steps toward her, stopping when I reach the desk. Looking across at her, I press my hands to the wood and lean forward. I'm practically breathing fire. "You sue us for unfair dismissal, and I'll haul your ass into court for breach of contract. You signed a contract, Morgan. And in that contract was a nondisclosure clause. Meaning you weren't allowed to tell the competition a single thing about what work you did here. The plus-sized line might have initially been your idea, but the moment you told it to me, on company time, in a meeting, it became Under Her's idea. And that, sweetheart, means you broke your contract. And I promise you this, by the time my lawyers are done with you, you'll be back to pouring coffee in Starbucks, where you fucking belong."

Have you ever hit someone?

I have. In grade school. I got in a fight with Thomas Purdy. He called me a faggot because my parents sold women's underwear for a living. Gotta love a kid's logic. Anyway, I clocked him right in the face. It was a good punch. But the point I'm getting to is, when I hit him—just right after my fist smashed into his face, and I pulled my hand away—there was this look in his eyes. Shock. Like he couldn't actually believe that I had just hit him.

That's the exact same look that Morgan has right now. Like she can't believe that I actually just said those words to her.

It was probably the same look I was wearing when she slapped me in Thailand.

Well, now, you know how it feels, baby.

Only I don't feel better for it.

And you know what's worse?

She doesn't react the way I expected her to.

I thought she'd tell me to fuck off. Yell at me. Maybe even slap me again.

But she does none of those things.

She presses her hands to her stomach, like she's in pain. Then, she straightens up, picks up her purse and cell phone from her desk, and walks straight past me and out of her office without saying a word.

38

Misery is lodged in my throat. Like my heart was trying to climb its way out of my body to escape the agony that'd been wrecking me since Morgan walked out of here yesterday, and on its way up, it got stuck in my throat, choking me ever since.

Have you ever seen that Mel Gibson film *Payback*? The one where Mel's character is betrayed by his wife and best friend for money. She shoots him in the back, and they both leave him for dead. Only he survives and goes after them for revenge.

Well, I'm kind of like Mel Gibson in that movie. Except I'm not a criminal, Morgan isn't my wife, she wasn't fucking my best friend, and she didn't shoot me in the back even though it feels like she did.

But what she did do was betray me.

Also, I'm not going to go after her for revenge. So, actually, scrap what I just said. It was a fucking stupid analogy.

But that's the theme of things with me at the moment when it comes to Morgan—stupid.

I pour more Jack into my glass and take a good gulp.

Yep. I'm drinking in my office during the day. Fucking sue me.

I hear a commotion outside my office. Then, my door is flying open, and a pint-sized woman with short, dark hair is barging into my office with Chrissy hot on her heels.

"Um, who are you?" God, even my voice sounds monotone.

It's so bad that I can't even muster up the energy to be pissed about a complete stranger just walking into my office, uninvited.

"I tried to stop her, Wilder. But she's pretty damn fast for a small person. She even managed to get past Leah."

I actually feel like raising a glass to this chick, whoever she is. She's definitely got some balls. Getting past Leah and Chrissy is no easy feat.

"I'm not small." She glares at Chrissy over her shoulder before looking back at me. "And my name is Joely Harper. I'm Morgan's best friend."

At the mention of Morgan, I feel like all the oxygen has just been sucked out of the room.

"Do you want me to toss her out on her ass?" Chrissy asks me.

Joely tosses a laugh over her shoulder. "I'd like to see you try."

Yep, she's definitely Morgan's friend.

And I need to get Chrissy out of here before a catfight breaks out in my office. "No. It's fine. She can stay. Can you close the door on your way out, please, Chrissy?"

Chrissy gives me a look of concern, and I give her a nod, telling her I'm fine.

She gives Joely one last angry stare and then walks out of my office.

"What can I do for you?" I ask Joely.

Under
HER

"Well, first off, you can pull your head out of your ass and go apologize to my best friend for breaking her heart and also for firing her."

I laugh. She's straight to the point; I've got to give her that.

"And the second thing?"

"After you're done apologizing for both of those things, then you can beg her for her forgiveness and give her, her job back."

I laugh again. This chick's a riot.

"Hang on…let me think about it." I tap my finger to my lips. "No. And no."

"You're a fucking idiot. You were an idiot in college, and apparently, you're an even bigger one now."

"And you're a bitch. And there's the door. Don't let it hit your ass on the way out." I down the rest of my whiskey and slam the glass on my desk.

She ignores me and comes over to my desk to take the seat across from me.

I blankly stare at her. "Do you have a hearing problem?"

"No, I can hear your bullshit just fine." She folds her arms over her chest. "Did you know Morgan was in love with you in college?"

My eyes snap up to hers. "Morgan hated me in college."

Joely unfolds her arms and leans forward. "Trust me, she was in love with you."

"So…why…" I shake my head, trying to clear my tangled thoughts.

"Why didn't she act like it? It's called self-preservation. But then you'd know a little something about that, right? Isn't that what you did yesterday when you tossed Morgan out of here? Because you thought she'd betrayed you? Isn't that what you're doing now while you sit here and tell yourself that you did the right thing by firing her? It's what we do when people hurt us. We go into defensive mode and protect ourselves in the only way we know how."

"You're right. People do that. But here's the thing. I never hurt Morgan in college. She just started hating on me for no fucking reason."

She laughs now. "It was thirteen years ago and eighteen-year-old Morgan's first term at Northwestern. She'd somehow landed the roommate from hell. Tori Watson. Ring any bells?"

I cast my mind back. Something is there, nagging in the back of my head, but I can't reach it properly to figure it out.

"No." I shake my head.

"Shame. I don't know if I'd have preferred that you did remember her. And what you both did to Morgan that night."

"I never did anything to Morgan," I growl. I don't like this chick's tone or the things she's implying.

"Morgan had just finished a shift at Starbucks. She came home and couldn't get in her room. Tori had locked her out because she was inside, hooking up with a guy. You." She points a finger at me. "Morgan eventually got her to open up the door. But Tori wouldn't let her in. Told her to find somewhere else to sleep. She spent the night on my dorm room floor."

"Bullshit. Morgan wouldn't have stood for that. She'd have told her to fuck off."

"The Morgan now—yeah, you're right; she would have. The Morgan back then? Not a chance. She just took it like she did."

"So, Tori locked her out. How is that my fault?"

"It's not. But you just stood there and said nothing—besides offering to let her join you and Tori."

I wince because that sounds exactly like something I would have said.

"You left Morgan with nowhere to sleep, which is shitty in itself. But it was what she heard you say after the door was closed that hurt her most."

"And what did I apparently say?"

"Basically, you said she was fat."

"Bullshit. I've never called a girl fat in my life."

"'Anything over a size four, and I show her the door.'"

Her words freeze in my ears. That was something Coop and I used to say when we were younger and fucking idiots.

But, no, I wouldn't have said that about Morgan. Would I have?

"Morgan wasn't fat in college."

"No, she wasn't. Not if you take the actual meaning of fat into context. But she wasn't exactly thin either. And, to morons like you and your frat buddies, she wasn't a size four or below; therefore, she was fat."

I swallow back, a sick feeling starting to swirl in my stomach.

"So, she hated me for something I said that I don't even remember saying. That's not exactly fair. And it doesn't excuse what she's done to me and my family's company."

"You're right; it wouldn't be fair. If she'd actually done any of those things that you accused her of."

"I saw the email."

"And I saw her devastation last night. Like I did all those years ago when you stood by and let a bunch of your frat buddies call her fat at a party. You did nothing, and then you went upstairs and screwed one of her best friends. But I'm guessing you don't remember that either."

I close my eyes and force my mind back.

"Hannah," I say, opening my eyes.

"Hannah," she echoes. "So, you do remember."

"But how was I to know? I didn't think Morgan gave a shit about me. I didn't know I was hurting her back then.

But she knew exactly what she was doing when she went to Coveted Lingerie with her idea—our idea."

"You know, Morgan wasn't going to tell me about what had happened with you and Hannah because she didn't want to cause problems between me and our so-called friend. But I know Morgan, and I knew something was wrong. It took me weeks to coax it out of her."

"I'm sorry about the thing with Hannah. But that was then, and this is now. She sold us out."

"Do you really believe that she would go behind your back like that?"

"I spoke to the supplier. I saw the—"

"Email. Yeah, you said. But you know what your problem is, Wilder? What your problem has always been when it comes to Morgan? You never saw her all those years ago. And you're still not seeing her now."

She gets up from the chair and walks toward my office door.

She pulls it open and then stops, turning back to me. "Don't make the same mistake again with her. Because I promise you, you will regret it."

39

I'm standing on the steps of Morgan's building, my finger hovering over the buzzer to her apartment.

It's been a day since Joely came barging into my office, giving me a piece of her mind.

And I've done a lot of thinking since then. In fact, it's all I've thought about, and the conclusion I've come to is...there's no way Morgan would have done this to me.

I know her.

And Joely was wrong when she said I didn't see Morgan. I do. I always did.

I was just an immature kid back then. I thought I knew who I was and what I wanted out of life. I accepted what Morgan had told me at face value instead of pushing her for answers.

Because, if I had done that, then we wouldn't have wasted the last thirteen years by not being together.

But, if Morgan had been more open with me, called me out on my dickish behavior, then I would have had to listen.

But she didn't. And here we are.

We're both to blame for the past. But this, right now…this is all me.

I didn't listen to her when she told me this wasn't her doing. I should have heard her and trusted her because she'd never given me a reason not to.

I should have known she wouldn't have done this.

We might have had our difficulties in the past. But one thing she never was, was cruel.

Unlike me.

I take a deep breath, ready to push the buzzer, when a window opens to my left, and the wrinkled, leathery face of an old lady stares back at me.

"Um, hi," I say.

"You a cold-caller?" She scowls.

"No, ma'am."

"You're not here to try to sell me Bibles, are you? Because, if I ain't found Jesus by now, then I ain't never gonna."

"Um…" I look down at my thousand-dollar suit, quite frankly insulted that she thinks I'm a Bible seller. "No, ma'am, I'm not here to sell Bibles."

"Then, what the hell are you doing, loitering on my doorstep?"

"I'm, uh, here to see Morgan."

Her eyes narrow on me. "Oh. You the boy who made my sweet girl Morgan cry?"

She must be the rottweiler neighbor that Morgan told me about. I forget what Morgan said her name was. On the few occasions when I stayed over here, I never saw her.

And never mind her being a rottweiler. She looks like Mama Fratelli from *The Goonies*. I'm half-expecting her to pull a gun on me and shoot me dead.

Basically, the woman is scary as shit.

"Um...yes, ma'am."

"You here to make her cry again?"

"Not if I can help it."

She glares at me for a long moment. I'm pretty sure she's trying to eviscerate me with her eyes.

Then, she disappears inside and shuts the window.

Okay.

A second later, the door buzzes open.

Guess Mama Fratelli isn't so bad after all.

I pull open the door and head inside. I'm halfway up the stairs when Mama Fratelli's voice stops me. I turn back and look at her.

"You make Morgan cry again, and you'll have me to deal with. I don't know if Morgan ever told you what I did for work before I retired. But I worked in the coroner's office, so I know how to get rid of a body without leaving any trace. You just keep that in mind, boy."

Nope. I was right the first time. She's frigging terrifying.

I'm pretty sure I just pissed my pants.

I swallow down. "Yes, ma'am."

She gives me a firm nod of her head. Then, she turns and shuffles back in her apartment.

Holy shit.

I blow out a breath as I turn and then jog up the stairs to Morgan's apartment.

When I reach her door, a minute later, I knock on it and wait.

I hear her soft footsteps coming up the hallway and toward the door, and my heart starts to thud.

"Mrs. Bigly, is that you?" she asks through the door.

Jesus, the sound of her voice...it's like a blade to my chest.

"No. It's me. Wilder."

There's silence behind the door, and for a moment, I think she isn't going to let me in. Then, I hear the sound of a chain being removed and the door unlocking. The door opens to reveal Morgan.

It's only been a few days since I last saw her, but it feels like it's been an eternity.

Her face is clean of makeup. Her eyes are puffy, like she's been crying—my fault.

Fuck, I'm an asshole.

Her hair is scraped back in a messy bun, and she's wearing an old Northwestern sweater with black leggings.

And she is still the most beautiful woman I have ever seen.

How did I live my life the last nine years without her in it? Actually, scrap that. How the fuck did I meet her thirteen years ago and not make her mine the very instant I laid eyes on her?

I'm a fucking moron.

"What do you want?" she says, her voice cold.

"To talk."

"If you're here to yell at me again, then you can just turn around and leave."

"I'm not here to yell. Just talk, I promise. Can I...come in?"

She hesitates, sizing me up with her eyes. Then, she steps back and moves aside, allowing me entry.

I step inside her apartment. As I pass her, the scent of her overwhelms me. So much so that I have to stop myself from grabbing her, wrapping my arms around her, burying my face in her hair, and begging for her forgiveness.

Somehow, I don't think that would be welcomed.

I need to apologize first. Tell her how I feel about her. And then, after that, if she still hasn't forgiven me, get to the begging part.

I follow Morgan into the living room.

"Can I get you something to drink?" she asks.

Even though I've been the world's biggest jerk, she's still polite enough to offer me a drink.

She's fucking perfect.

And I'm an idiot.

"Water would be great, thanks."

I take a seat on the sofa while I wait for her to come back.

She appears a few minutes later.

"Thanks," I say when she hands me the water.

She sits in the chair across from me. I take a sip of water and then put it down on the coffee table.

I'm not really a guy who gets nervous. Right now, I'm nervous.

I lean forward, arms on my thighs, and I clasp my hands together as I look her in the face. "I'm sorry, Morgan," I say. "So fucking sorry. For everything. For a couple of days ago. For accusing you of going to Coveted Lingerie and for the shitty things I said. I know you didn't go to them and sell them the idea."

"How do you know?" she bats back at me.

"Because I know *you*. I let the evidence override what I'd already known—that you would never do something like that to the company...to me."

"How do you know that? You've only known me for a month."

"I've known you for thirteen years. We might have spent most of those years apart, but I knew you in college, and I know you now."

She laughs, and it sounds bitter. "You didn't know me in college."

"Actually, no, you're right. I didn't know all of you in college, not like I do now. Back then, I only knew what you allowed me to know. And I know that's my fault, too."

A question flickers in her eyes, so I answer, "Your friend Joely came to see me yesterday." I see a multitude of emotions cross her face, one of them worry.

"What did she say to you?"

"Things I needed to hear. And some things that you should have told me."

"Such as?"

"How you had feelings for me in college. How I hurt you on numerous occasions because I was a stupid, immature kid. I'm sorry for Tori and Hannah"—she winces, and I feel sick—"and for the shitty things I did and said."

Her expression shuts down. "I don't want to go over the past."

"We need to go over the past," I tell her. "All these years, I thought you hated me back in college. I thought you were judgmental, but that wasn't the case, was it? You were just protecting yourself."

She nods her head.

"Talk to me," I say gently.

She closes her eyes, like she can't look at me and say the words. "I had a crush on you back then." She opens her eyes but doesn't look at me. "And, of course, seeing you with Tori hurt, but I can't blame you for that because you didn't know how I felt. But you said…" Her lip trembles.

"I never thought you were fat, babe."

She winces, and I want to go back in time and punch the idiot kid that I was in the face. "I know what I said, and it was a dickish, stupid thing to say. I was a dumb kid, and I hurt the one person who never deserved to be hurt."

"But it wasn't just that. You stood by while your friends said mean things about me, and you never once said anything to stop them."

"I hate that I did that. I hate that I don't even remember. I can't change the past. All I can do is try to make up for it and apologize for my dickish behavior back then…and now."

"You slept with my friend Hannah."

"I know." I scrub my hands over my face.

"I know you had no clue how I felt about you in college, but I always felt invisible to you, and I put that down to you thinking that…I wasn't good enough for you. And I still feel the same."

"Fuck no."

I'm off the sofa, kneeling at her feet, grabbing hold of her hands. She doesn't hold mine back, but she doesn't push me away either, so I take that as a good thing.

"I'm not good enough for you. I wasn't back then. And I'm not now. But I'm selfish enough to tell you that I'm in love with you. I fucking love you, Morgan, and I need you."

Tears are glistening in her eyes, and I don't know if that's a good thing or a bad thing, so I keep going.

"I am madly and crazy in love with you, and I need you to forgive me because I don't know how to get through another day without you."

She's not saying anything, and I've never been so afraid in my whole life.

"Morgan?"

"You hurt me. And I'm not just talking about the past. That's over and done. The moment I let you kiss me in Thailand, I decided it was time to let all of that go. I thought you'd changed. That's why I let myself fall for you again. But, that last day in my office…the things you said…"

"I'm so sorry," I beg. "So fucking sorry." Panic is filling my chest, and I'm ashamed to admit there are tears in my eyes.

"You thought I was capable of betraying you like that."

"I reacted badly. I know."

"That's an understatement. What you said…" Her eyes fill with tears, and I hate that I'm the one who put them there. "I don't think I can trust you with my feelings anymore."

She slips her hands from mine.

The panic inside me fills to full-blown fear. "Please, baby. I fucked up, and I'm so sorry. Just don't throw us away."

"I didn't. You did. A couple of days ago."

I've lost her. And I don't know what to do.

"Please, babe. I made a mistake then. I've made too many mistakes when it comes to you. But I'm willing to do anything to fix things between us. I just…I need you. The company needs you. Neither of us will survive without you."

She closes her eyes and blows out a breath. "Wilder…I can't come back to work…not now."

Because of me.

"The company's yours."

"What?" Her eyes pop open.

At first, I'm shocked, too, that I said it. But then it's suddenly so clear. I know it's the right thing to do. The way to show her that I'm sorry and how much she means to me is to give her the one thing that has always meant the most to me. Because, when I compare the two—Morgan and the business—there is no comparison. She wins out every time.

"The company is yours. You can run it alone as CEO."

"Wilder…no. Why would you do that?"

"Because I love you. Because the company needs you. You're the best thing that has ever happened to Under Her. You're the best thing that has ever happened to me. I know I fucked us up, but I won't be the reason you walk away from the company. You're amazing at your job. Look at how much you've done in such a short time."

"And look what happened. The deal went south."

"But it can be fixed. I know it can. And, if anyone can sort it out, it's you."

She bites her lip and stares past me. The silence that hangs between us is killing me.

"Maybe…but I don't want to do it alone," she says quietly.

And my heart stops.

"What are you saying?"

"I'm saying"—she blows out a breath—"that you messed up. But so have I." Her eyes come to mine. "I never told you back in college how I felt. Or that you hurt me. I never gave you the chance to apologize or make it right. I just shut down on you."

"If I hadn't said or done those things, then—"

She silences me with her fingers to my lips. "I know. But it's in the past. I want it to stay there. And, the other day…you screwed up big time, but I can understand why you thought it was me. You should have trusted me at my word, but I understand why you jumped to the wrong conclusion."

I take hold of her hand and slip her fingers across my lips. "So, you forgive me?"

She shrugs. "I guess…but you've got some serious making up to do, Cross."

"Are we talking making up to do as co-CEOs or…me as your boyfriend?"

She pauses a moment, lips pursed, like she's thinking it over. Then, she smiles. "Both," she says.

And my heart soars.

I take her face in my hands and stare into her eyes. "You won't regret this. I swear."

"I'd better not. This is your last chance, Wilder."

And I can't wait a second longer. I kiss her.

She immediately kisses me back, and the feeling is amazing. I never want to come close to losing her ever again.

"I love you," I say against her lips. "So fucking much."

"I love you, too," she whispers.

I jerk my head back. "You do?"

She smiles. "Of course I do, dummy."

A big smile spreads across my face. "So, this making up I've got to do…I'm thinking I should get started on the boyfriend part of it."

Fire ignites in her eyes. "Oh, yeah?"

"Yeah." I pick her up, making her squeal, and I carry her to her bed and drop her on it.

Then, I climb on top of her and get to work on making it up to my girl.

Epilogue

So, I guess you're wondering who told Coveted Lingerie about our plus-sized launch and the deal with Ananda along with who made the call and sent the email to Niran, pretending to be Morgan.

Didn't take a genius to figure it out.

Well, not that it was me who figured it out, of course. That was all Morgan.

Anyway, it was Sierra.

She'd discovered that Morgan and I were sleeping together. God knows how, as we had been careful around the office, but she'd found out, and she had been less than happy about it, so she'd decided to get back at us by screwing up the Ananda deal. And maybe she'd thought that, by trying to make it out that Morgan had told Coveted, it would break us up and leave the way clear for Sierra.

When Morgan and I confronted Sierra with our suspicions, she denied it at first. But, when Morgan told her that it was her login that signed into the system a few minutes before the email was sent to Niran, using Morgan's email that Sierra had access to, she folded like a deck of cards.

Turns out, Sierra's cousin works in the marketing department at Coveted Lingerie, and she was looking for a foot up the career ladder, so Sierra gave her one. Two birds, one stone.

Fair to say, she was fired on the spot and escorted from the building.

Because there was nothing to be done about the deal with Ananda, as Niran had done what he had to so that he could keep his business afloat, we had to find another supplier.

It wasn't easy. But Morgan and I worked all our contacts and barely slept until we found one in Bangkok. The silk was more expensive than Ananda but still cheaper than our Chinese supplier. The sales margin would be low, but they promised us early delivery, which meant we could launch before Coveted.

It was a risk, but it was one that paid off.

The product flew off the shelves.

Mainly thanks to the design team and artist that Morgan had brought in. Zoey Marchant is a friend of Morgan's. They had met at yoga class a few years ago. She's an artist, a starving artist, but her work is amazing. Morgan had asked her if she'd like to design the prints for the bras.

She'd said yes, and the rest is history.

My parents were thrilled with how Morgan and I'd brought this back around and made such a success out of it when it could have just failed after Coveted took our idea and supplier.

Morgan says it's because of both of us, but I say it's all her. I couldn't have done it without her. I wouldn't be the man I am now without her.

And my parents are also thrilled that Morgan and I are together. There was no keeping our relationship under

Under HER

wraps after the whole Sierra thing, and honestly, I didn't want to. I wanted everyone to know that this smart, beautiful woman was mine.

I do have to wonder if that was part of my mom's plan when she brought Morgan in to work at Under Her. Not that she didn't bring her talent to the company because she's smart as hell, and she could run it with her eyes closed. But maybe it was also to give me a counterpart—not only in business, but in my personal life, too.

In business, I was a grown-ass man, but in my private life, I was still acting like a teenager.

But not now. I'm a different man now. Because of Morgan. She's changed me for the better.

I'm a man in love. And love will do some crazy things to you.

Things I wouldn't change for the world.

So, life is fucking great. I've got the most incredible woman by my side at work and in my bed at night.

My parents and friends love her. Mom, Dad, Coop, and Dom think the sun shines out of Morgan's ass—well, it does—but I do sometimes think they like her more than me. If they do, they should. She's a far better person than I could ever hope to be.

I just thank God that she sees something in me and wants to be with me. Because, without her, the company and I would be nothing.

And the company has been selling product faster than we can supply it, thanks to Morgan's genius, and our Bangkok supplier can't meet all of our demands. As Ananda only signed with Coveted for the initial batch they stole from us, they are free to sign with us again. So, we now have both our Bangkok supplier and Ananda for the plus-sized range. As the range has brought in new customers for our standard sizes, too, I feel that, soon, I'm going to be asking Niran if expansion is an option.

Speaking of Niran, Morgan and I are back in San Kamphaeng, staying at the Secret Garden Chiang Mai. We're not here to work though. We're here on vacation. It's been one year since she slapped me, since I kissed the shit out of her, and since we came back here before I gave her a ride on the Wilder side.

I know, I know. Cheesy as fuck. But I just couldn't resist.

I thought it would be romantic to bring her here for our anniversary, and it turned out, I was right. When I gave her the tickets for our vacation, she got this soft look in her eyes. And, that night, I got the mother of all blow jobs. I'm talking deep-throat, porn-star action.

It was frigging amazing.

And, right now, we're lying in bed together, both covered in sweat, panting to catch our breaths.

I thought it would be a good idea to reenact our first night together, minus the slap across the face. So, we went to the Hot Springs and then to the same bar, except we actually ate this time. Then, we came back here, and I was undressing her before she even got the door open.

"Wow," she says.

"I know."

"It gets better every time, right? It's not just me?"

I turn on my side to face her and brush her hair off her forehead. "It's not just you, babe. It's us together. We're fucking dynamite in the sack."

She giggles, and of course, my cock reacts. She breathes, and he reacts.

It's gotten incredibly difficult to get through staff meetings with her and not get a stiffy.

She's amazing, and she's all mine.

She moves to get up, and I pull her back down to me.

"Where are you going?"

"To clean up."

"We'll get a shower together."

"We didn't do that on the first night."

"No, we didn't, but then I didn't ask you to move in with me either that night, so I guess we're adding a new memory to our anniversary."

She's staring at me, not saying anything, with a shock and dazed look in her eyes.

I smile and say, "If you didn't get that the first time, that was me, Wilder Cross, asking you, Morgan Stickford, to move in with me."

Her lips part. She licks them. "You want me to move in with you?"

"Yes. We can live at my place or yours, or we can buy somewhere new together."

"But that means, we'd be working together and living together. Are you sure that's what you want?"

"Babe, I know what I want—you all the time. You're the only person I can spend this much time around, and it still doesn't feel like enough. We're practically living together already. We stay over at each other's places all the time. Question is, is it what you want?"

I hold my breath, waiting for her answer.

Then, she smiles, and it's beautiful. "Of course it's what I want."

She throws her arms around my neck, hugging me, and I hold her back just as tight.

"Best anniversary gift ever," she whispers. "But I feel bad. I didn't get you anything. You said, no gifts."

"You're my gift, babe." And she is.

"Still, I want to give you something," she murmurs. She starts to kiss her way down my body.

Who am I to argue if my girl wants to gift me a blow job?

And, if the last blow job after I gave her the tickets to come here is anything to go by, then think of the sucking I'm in for after asking her to move in with me.

Fuck, I wonder what I'll get when I ask her to be Mrs. Cross.

And, yes, I said *when*, not *if*.

But that's not for now. That's for another time…in the not-so-distant future.

I'd say…a year from now.

But, right now, I'm going to just enjoy the hell out of living with Morgan, my partner in work and life.

Morgan Stickford, the girl who used to hate loving me.

Who now just loves me.

The End

Acknowledgments

There's a bunch of fantabulous people who I couldn't do this without. As always, first is my husband, Craig, who goes through every single step of writing a book with me, and I couldn't do it without him. And my children, who are the best kids a mom could wish for.

Lauren Abramo, best agent ever! You continue to bring amazing things to the table, and you support every single decision I make.

My girls—Jodi, Trishy, and Sali. Best book friends a girl could ask for.

Jovana, my editor, who always manages to find time to fit me in when I drop a last-minute book on her. You polished this book to perfection. Thank you.

And thanks to my girl Naj for yet another stunning cover.

My Wether Girls, I seriously heart our group.

A big thank-you to all the bloggers who work tirelessly to help promote books. I appreciate and adore you all.

And, lastly, to my fabulous readers—Your continuing support makes it possible for me to do what I love. My biggest thank-you of all goes to each and every one of you.

About the Author

SAMANTHA TOWLE is a *New York Times*, *USA Today*, and *Wall Street Journal* best-selling author. She began her first novel in 2008 while on maternity leave. She completed the manuscript five months later and hasn't stopped writing since.

She is the author of contemporary romances, The Storm Series and The Revved Series, and stand-alones, *Trouble*, *When I Was Yours*, *The Ending I Want*, *Unsuitable*, *Wardrobe Malfunction*, and *Sacking the Quarterback*, which was written with James Patterson. She has also written paranormal romances, *The Bringer* and The Alexandra Jones Series. All of her books are penned to the tunes of The Killers, Kings of Leon, Adele, The Doors, Oasis, Fleetwood Mac, Lana Del Rey, and more of her favorite musicians.

SAMANTHA TOWLE

A native of Hull and a graduate of Salford University, she lives with her husband, Craig, in East Yorkshire with their son and daughter.

Printed in Great Britain
by Amazon